Praise for Kate Hoffmann
from *RT Book Reviews*

The Charmer
"Hoffmann's deeply felt, emotional story is
riveting. It's impossible to put down."

Your Bed or Mine?
"Fully developed characters and perfect pacing
make this story feel completely right."

Doing Ireland!
"Sexy and wildly romantic."

The Mighty Quinns: Ian
"A very hot story mixes with great characters
to make every page a delight."

Who Needs Mistletoe?
"Romantic, sexy and heartwarming."

The Mighty Quinns: Teague
"Sexy, heartwarming and romantic...a story to
settle down with and enjoy—and then re-read."

Blaze

Dear Reader,

Welcome to the second book in my Mighty Quinns trilogy, featuring youngest brother, Danny.

About ten years ago, I happened across a small blacksmith shop near my hometown and decided to stop in and see what was going on. I'd nearly forgotten that place until I was looking for a profession for Danny Quinn and it just popped into my head.

I was so impressed by an artist using fire and tools to coax beautiful shapes from reluctant iron. It took strength and patience and creativity—exactly the qualities I wanted for Danny.

I hope you enjoy *The Mighty Quinns: Danny.* And don't miss the final book in the trilogy next month, when eldest brother, Kellan, meets his match.

Happy reading,

Kate Hoffmann

Kate Hoffmann

THE MIGHTY QUINNS: DANNY

TORONTO NEW YORK LONDON
AMSTERDAM PARIS SYDNEY HAMBURG
STOCKHOLM ATHENS TOKYO MILAN MADRID
PRAGUE WARSAW BUDAPEST AUCKLAND

Recycling programs
for this product may
not exist in your area.

ISBN-13: 978-0-373-79651-9

THE MIGHTY QUINNS: DANNY

ABOUT THE AUTHOR

Kate Hoffmann began writing for Harlequin Books in 1993. Since then she's published sixty-five books, primarily in the Harlequin Temptation and Harlequin Blaze lines. When she isn't writing, she enjoys music, theater and musical theater. She is active working with high school students in the performing arts. She lives in southeastern Wisconsin with her cat, Chloe.

Books by Kate Hoffmann

To get the inside scoop on Harlequin Blaze and its talented writers, be sure to check out blazeauthors.com.

Don't miss any of our special offers. Write to us at the following address for information on our newest releases.

Harlequin Reader Service
U.S.: 3010 Walden Ave., P.O. Box 1325, Buffalo, NY 14269
Canadian: P.O. Box 609, Fort Erie, Ont. L2A 5X3

Prologue

DANNY QUINN PULLED the pocketknife from his jacket and opened the blade. He carefully cut into the piece of soap he'd stolen from beneath the kitchen sink, hoping his mother wouldn't notice it was missing before he had a chance to finish his carving.

A brisk breeze blew off the sea, scattering the flakes of soap in the sand. He'd come down to his favorite spot, a spot he'd named Smuggler's Cove, to get away from his brothers. There weren't many places the youngest Quinn had all to his own, but this was one of them.

He'd spent a lot of solitary time in the area. Beyond the cliffs was the old haunted castle, a place his older brothers always talked about. He hadn't quite gathered the courage to venture inside; but he had found this spot, far enough from the ghosts and goblins that guarded the old tower. Though it was a five-kilometer walk cross-country, it was worth it to put distance between him and his tormentors.

Today, just after breakfast, he had sneaked away from home, his rucksack packed with a lunch, scraps of driftwood and soap and his pocketknife—ready to enjoy a day alone. Who needed older brothers anyhow? He was just grand on his own.

"I saw him go down here!"

Danny looked up to see his eldest brother, Kellan, standing thirty feet above him. He scrambled back to hide himself against the rocks, but he wasn't fast enough. "He's down at the bottom," Kellan shouted.

"Go away," Danny yelled. "This is my place and you can't come down."

"How did you get down there?" Kellan called.

"I jumped," Danny shot back.

Riley appeared beside Kellan. It was now two against one, the typical breakdown between the three brothers. "Bollocks!" Riley said. "Tell us how you got down or we'll tell Ma you were climbing on the cliffs."

They wouldn't go away. His older brothers were merciless. "Find the rock that looks like a duck," Danny finally said. "The path is on the other side of that." He watched as Riley and Kellan searched for the right spot and then slowly descended through the rocks. As they both leapt down onto the sand, Danny watched them warily.

"How did you find this place?" Kellan asked, looking around in wonder.

"I was searching for driftwood in the rocks. I just found it." He cursed. "How did you find me?"

"We followed you," Kellan said, a wide grin on his face. "We were curious where you were off to in such a rush."

"What are you doin' down here?" Riley asked. He pointed to the bar of soap that Danny held to his chest. "What's that? Are you plannin' on a bath, then? Tryin' to smell grand for your girlfriend, Evelyn?" Riley laughed, jabbing Kellan in the side with his elbow. "That's why he's hidin' out here. Danny has a sweetheart. Maybe she's meetin' him here for a bit of snogging."

"You in love with Evelyn, Danno?" Kellan asked, circling around him.

"No," Danny muttered. "I don't have a girl."

"Then why are you holdin' so tight to that soap?" Riley asked.

Danny tried to shove it in his jacket pocket, but Kellan was waiting to snatch it from his grip. Danny cursed as his brother retreated a safe distance.

"What are you doing with this?" Kellan said with a laugh, looking down at the dragon's head that Danny had begun to carve. He immediately went silent. Riley frowned, then walked over to Kellan's side. "What is it?"

"Where did you get this?" Kellan asked.

"It's mine," Danny murmured. "Now give it over."

"Who did you steal this from?" Kellan demanded.

"No one. I told you, it's mine."

Riley held up the soap, pointing to the dragon's head. "You carved this?"

"I did," Danny said, grabbing the soap back from his brother.

"Shut yer gob," Riley said. "You can't carve like that. You're just a baby."

Danny's eyes narrowed. "I'm eight years old."

"Prove it," Riley challenged. "Prove you carved that."

"I don't have to do anything you tell me," Danny said. "You're not my da, so feck off, the both of you."

"Maybe he did," Kellan said. "He's a clever little shite. After all, he found this place, didn't he?"

"I did," Danny insisted. "And I'll show you." Plopping down on the sand, he opened his rucksack and began to pull out all the carvings he'd done in the past few months. His collection was always changing—some he kept, some he gave to school chums and some he threw into the sea when they looked too crude against the others.

Riley and Kellan watched him, silently, suspiciously. But as his menagerie of animals and insects and mythic creatures grew, they leaned in more closely. "Will you look at that," Kellan murmured. He reached out and picked up a beetle that Danny was particularly proud of, carved out of a palm-sized piece of driftwood. "How do you do this?"

"I have to find a good piece of wood first," Danny explained. "Then I stare at it for a while, and pretty soon I see what I want to carve. Then, I just take away everything that isn't the beetle. My teacher says that's how the great sculptors do it."

"Look at this," Riley said, grabbing a dinosaur. "He's even got the spikes on the tail."

They sat down on either side of him and examined all of Danny's carvings, their comments filled with awe and respect for his talents. This was the first time in his whole life that his brothers had taken him seriously. Usually, they just ignored him and left him behind. But now, he could do something they couldn't. And that was like gold.

"Would you like one, then?" Danny asked.

His brothers looked at each other. "We can have one?"

"Sure," he said. "Any one you like."

"Can ya make me something?" Kellan asked.

Danny nodded. "I can. If you find a picture, I can carve it." He rummaged in his rucksack until he found the photo he'd torn out of a magazine. "I'm going to make this troll for Ma's garden, for her birthday, but I have to find a big piece of wood."

"We'll help you find one," Riley said. "There's got to be a good piece around here somewhere."

He and his brothers searched the beach for a long time, climbing over the rocks and talking about Danny's carvings. It was the best day of Danny's whole life, better than any day he could remember. Somehow, he knew things had changed, that he was someone important to Riley and Kellan now. The duo was now a trio.

"I can show you something else," Danny offered. "It's a secret and you can't tell Da or Ma or they'll take the strap to us all. And you can't tell anyone else. None of your friends. It has to be for Quinn brothers only."

"We swear," Kellan said.

"You have to make a blood oath," Danny said. He opened his pocketknife and held out his hand. Without flinching, he cut the tip of his index finger, then handed the knife to Riley. "Do it," he said. "Or I won't tell you."

Reluctantly, both Kellan and Riley cut their fingers, then let the blood drip onto their palms. Then the three brothers grasped hands, mingling their blood. Riley grinned at Kellan. "He's a brave little bugger, isn't he?"

"Let's see it," Kellan said, drawing his hand away.

"It's a cave," Danny said. "In the cliff. It's deep and

I didn't go all the way in because the tide comes up into the opening. But I think that smugglers might have used it." He pulled a tiny flashlight out of his jacket pocket and turned it on. "We've only got an hour before the tide starts coming in. We'll have to hurry."

"Are you sure we should do this?" Riley said. "What if it's dangerous?"

Danny gave him a look. "If you're afraid, you can stay on the beach."

As he walked across the sand to the rocky outcropping, Danny smiled to himself. Though he was only eight, he felt like a full-grown man. Maybe now, he'd have enough courage to talk to Evelyn Maltby.

1

"So THIS IS BALLYKIRK," Jordan Kennally murmured to herself, peering through the windshield of her car at the picturesque village below.

She'd been in Ireland for nearly sixteen months now, working as the project manager on the Castle Cnoc renovation. And though she'd seen a lot of the countryside, she was still amazed at how every sight managed to look exactly like some picture-postcard. Ireland was nothing if not quaint.

She glanced at the clock on the dash, then calculated the time it would take her to find Danny Quinn, discuss their business and get back to the castle. She wasn't used to chasing around the countryside looking for workers, but she'd been told that Danny Quinn was the best. And Jordan needed the best.

She steered her car down the winding road that led into Ballykirk, following the carefully drawn map that Kellan Quinn had provided. The town was like so many others along the coast of County Cork—a pretty collection of colorful buildings set against a stunning landscape, this time the blue waters of Bantry Bay.

When her father had assigned her the project at Castle Cnoc, she'd looked at it as both punishment and reward. It was her first project as manager, solely in charge of a five-million-dollar budget and pleasing one of her father's wealthy clients. It was also a way of putting her firmly into her place at Kencor.

She'd been doggedly scratching her way up the corporate ladder of her family's multimillion dollar real estate development firm, working hard to carve out a place for herself. But with four equally driven and talented older brothers above her on the ladder, just the process of getting noticed was impossible.

She'd begged for good projects to manage, but had always been given a secondary role, usually as the interior designer, for projects that her brothers headed. She'd been sent to Ireland to oversee the restoration of a once grand manor house and castle keep, because no one else could be bothered to come. They were all too busy with hotels and shopping malls and office towers.

"Whistler Cottage." No street, no number, just a name. Jordan studied the map. "Behind the bakery and up the hill to the blue cottage," she read. The bakery was easy enough to find and when she did, Jordan parked her car, grabbed her bag and jumped out of the vehicle.

There were blacksmiths scattered all over Ireland, their skills ranging from amateur to competent artisan. But Danny Quinn was known as one of the best ornamental blacksmiths in the country, a true artist, and she intended to hire him for her project.

His brother, Kellan, had served as the architect on the Castle Cnoc restoration and Jordan had assumed that Danny would jump at a big-budget job so close to home. But he hadn't returned any of her calls. So Jordan had decided to force the issue. She needed an answer, one way or another, or she'd be put off schedule.

The pressure to bring the job in on time and under budget was immense. If she did, her father wouldn't be able to ignore her anymore. The next logical step would be the boutique hotel they were developing in SoHo and after that, progressively larger projects. They wouldn't think of her as the company "decorator" anymore.

Jordan cursed softly. They all looked at her like some swatch-wielding cream puff, unable to exert any power with the mostly male contractors on the job sites. Maybe she didn't curse and throw tantrums and berate the workers, but that didn't mean she didn't get the job done. Jordan had always preferred a quiet confidence to a raging temper. You get more flies with honey. That's what her grandmother had always said.

But she'd been pleasant to Danny Quinn, polite on all the messages she'd left. Maybe it was time to get tough. If he didn't want the job, he needed to tell her outright so she could find someone else. Trouble was, she didn't want anyone else. Kellan had shown her a portfolio of his brother's work and Danny was exactly who she needed to provide some of the authentic details she sought for the project.

As the map indicated, a cobblestone path led between the bakery and the adjacent building. After walking through a narrow alleyway, she saw the sign for the smithy—a decorative iron anvil and tongs attached to the side of an azure cottage set on the low hillside.

The front door to the cottage was wide open and she walked inside. Two black-and-white dogs lying near the fireplace immediately leapt up and began barking at her. They scampered across the room, driving her against a battered breakfront.

"Shh," she urged, working her way back to the front door. "Settle down. I'm not going to hurt you." Jordan held out her hand as she made her retreat. But just as she turned to step outside, she ran face-first into a wide, muscular and naked chest.

A tiny cry slipped from her lips as she stumbled back. The dogs got behind her legs and she felt herself losing her balance. And then she was on the floor with the dogs climbing all over her, licking at her face and nuzzling her hands.

"Finny. Mogue. Away now."

The dogs retreated a safe distance, then sat down and peered at her with curious blue eyes, their tongues hanging out, their heads cocked. They looked so pleased with themselves. "Thank you so much for the lovely welcome," she muttered to the dogs as she struggled to her feet. A moment later, the man grabbed her hand and helped her up. It was only then that Jordan got a good look at the elusive Danny Quinn.

The family resemblance was keen. At first glance, he looked like his older brother, Kellan. But upon more careful study, she saw that where Kellan was handsome in a cool, sophisticated way, his brother oozed raw sex appeal.

He wore torn blue jeans that rode low on his narrow hips, and an old work shirt, open at the front and missing its sleeves. A sheen of perspiration covered his sinewy arms and chest. His hair, nearly black, stood up in unruly spikes. But it was his eyes, pale blue in color, that caught her complete attention. She forced herself to look away and her gaze drifted to a narrow strip of hair that traced a line from his navel to beneath his—

"Sorry about the dogs," he said with a boyish smile. "They'll herd anything that moves." He paused. "How they could mistake you for a sheep, I'll never know."

Jordan looked up, her face warming with embarrassment. Sheep? What was she doing? Quinn was a business associate. "You—you must be Daniel Quinn."

"I must be," he said. "And who must you be?"

"Oh." She held out her hand. "Jordan. Jordan Kennally."

He seemed taken aback by her introduction, but then wiped his hand on his jeans and took her fingers in his. "You're Joe Kennally?"

"Jordan," she said. "Your brother calls me Joe. He thinks it's funny." She cleared her throat, determined to stay on the subject at hand. "I've been trying to contact you for the past two weeks now and haven't gotten a call back. So I decided a visit was in order." He stared at her silently. "What?" she asked, an impatient edge to her voice.

"I'm just surprised you're a girl. Kell neglected to mention that."

Jordan felt her temper rise. That comment had been thrown at her regularly since she'd begun working for her father's development company. Why couldn't she be a girl? Women had every right to work in the construction industry these days. And Jordan wasn't a name reserved exclusively for boys.

"Is that a problem?" she asked, snatching her hand

back and fixing him with a cool look. Obviously, the only way to keep this conversation on track was to present a tough facade.

Danny shrugged. "I can assure you, that's never been a problem with me. And had I known you were a woman, I might not have dodged your calls for two weeks." He chuckled. "And had I known that you were so beautiful, I'd have turned up on your doorstep in less than a day."

"You could tell I was a woman from the messages," she said.

Danny frowned. "I really wasn't paying attention. I usually just ignore my phone messages."

"That's always a good business practice," she murmured.

He stepped out of the door and motioned for her to follow him. "Come on then, I'll show you around."

To her consternation, he didn't bother to button up his shirt and she found herself fixated on that thin line of hair, this time following it up from his belly to his collarbone. Maybe she should offer him a chance to put on something more appropriate for a business meeting. When her attention shifted to the sculpted muscles of his upper arms, Jordan stifled a groan.

She stepped past him, her shoulder brushing against his body as she walked outside. The contact sent another current racing through her. Jordan wanted to scream. What was happening to her? After just a few minutes, this man had her completely off balance. There was no way she'd be able to negotiate a contract with him in this state. He could ask for a million Euros and her naked body in his bed and she'd sign on the dotted line.

"Just follow the path to the back," he said, pointing.

Since she'd been in Ireland, Jordan had lived the life of a nun. The first year, she'd made a point to return to New York at least once a month, in an attempt to maintain a romantic relationship with her last boyfriend. But after their breakup, it had seemed like a waste of time and money.

Though she'd made a few acquaintances in the area, she'd kept to herself. In truth, she wasn't very good with friends. Work always took precedence and she often turned down invitations to socialize because of that. She put all her energy into her job.

"Did your brother tell you about the project?" she asked as they walked to a small stone barn set behind the cottage.

"I know the place," Danny replied. "Castle Cnoc. We used to go out there when we were teenagers. It was a grand spot for a party if you could avoid getting caught by the peelers."

"Peelers?"

"The gardai. The…cops. People around here think it's haunted, you know."

"Yes, well, a lot has changed," she said, risking a sideways glance. "We've finished with most of the renovations. But we still have a lot of the details to get right. Your brother showed me your portfolio. I like your work. A lot of the original ironwork was stripped out of the place after it was abandoned, but we do have photos from early in the twentieth century and some samples we managed to find. So you'd do some new fabrication and some restoration of existing work. We want to put everything back the way it was."

"It's a big job of work," he said. "That place is huge."

"We haven't done anything to the castle itself. That will be done later. It's the attached manor house that we're working on."

"That's still a big house," he said. "And the last time I saw it, it was a ruin."

"Nine bedrooms. Nearly ten thousand square feet. Built in 1860 with a major addition in 1910. I know we haven't talked money, but I figured you'd want to see what's required before you give me a quote. And I wanted to meet you, to see if we…well, if we could work together."

They reached the door to the old stone barn and he stopped and stood in front of her, staring at her in a brazen way. She pressed her hand to her chest, wondering why her heart was suddenly beating so fast. Was it the smile that made his mouth seem more kissable? Or was it the sheen of perspiration that made her long to touch his bare skin? Or was it—

"So, this is kind of like a first date for us," he commented. "We're just feeling each other out, trying to decide whether we want to get involved, is that it?"

Jordan felt her cheeks blaze again. This was crazy! She'd dealt with handsome men like Danny Quinn all her adult life. What was it about him that had turned her into a silly teenager? "It's purely a business transaction, Mr. Quinn. It has nothing to do with my feelings for you. Not that I have any feelings at all for you. We just met."

"Oh." He nodded. "Then it would be more like I'm a brasser and you're my customer?"

"A brasser?"

"A prostitute? A hooker, I think you Americans call it."

"I'm not making you do anything illegal, unless making hinges and gates will get you arrested in Ireland."

"You haven't seen my hinges," he said with a grin. "They're obscenely sexy. Erotic, some would say."

She had to put a stop to this—this playful, but highly suggestive banter. "Mr. Quinn, I—"

"Oh, Jaysus, can we stop with the Mr. Quinn? No one ever calls me mister. And it makes you sound like a snootypants."

"Do you want this job?" she asked, her eyes narrowing in frustration. "Because I get the feeling you're doing everything in your power to get me to turn around and walk back to my car."

He raked his hand through his tousled hair. "Now don't be doing that. I'm just having a bit of fun," he cajoled. "And you're right, I'm not really sure I want to take on a job like this. Copying someone else's work doesn't appeal to my creative sensibilities at all."

"But you'd be a part of a really wonderful project. The castle is going to be restored to its former grandeur."

"Why? So some rich American can live there and pretend he's a nineteenth-century lord, looking down on all the locals? Oh, count me in on that. And while you're at it, do you have a few red-hot pokers you'd like to stick in my eye?"

Jordan stared at him, baffled by his response. She'd gotten the impression from Kellan that his brother really needed the work. But it was clear that Danny Quinn required more than just a decent paycheck before he took a job. He needed inspiration.

"So who is it that bought the old castle?" he asked. "Everyone in the county has been speculating. Whoever it is must have money to burn."

"I'm really not at liberty to—"

"If you expect me to take the job, I'm going to want to know who I'm working for."

"You'd be working for me," Jordan said.

"And who would you be working for?" He pointed inside the barn. "After you."

She opened her mouth to counter his sarcastic query, but as soon as her eyes adjusted to the dark interior of the barn, Jordan was silenced. From every rafter, in every nook and cranny, there were beautiful objects made of iron, twisted into shapes she'd never thought possible. She saw gates and railings and balustrades and a beautiful sundial that she immediately wanted for the garden at Castle Cnoc.

But it wasn't just architectural items that she found. Along one wall were a series of small animals, hedgehogs and rabbits and squirrels, clever little creatures made of cast iron. She wandered over to a crooked shelf tacked to a crossbeam and examined a collection of small carved objects.

"You did these?" she asked, glancing over her shoulder.

"When I was a kid. The cast-iron animals are for the tourists. They're small enough to fit in a suitcase and make a nice remembrance. You wouldn't believe how many good jobs I get because of those bloody hedgehogs."

Jordan smiled. "They are cute."

He reached down and grabbed one and handed it to her. "Then take one with you. They make a proper doorstop or a decent paperweight. But they're pure hell if your toe runs across one in the dark."

"Thank you," Jordan said.

He stared at her for a long moment. "You have a lovely smile," Danny said.

Jordan quickly turned away, crossing the dirt floor to the forge. The massive stone fireplace, set at waist level, was located against the far wall, banked with coal, red embers glowing inside. Soot stained the stone above the hearth. Tools lined the walls surrounding the forge and a battered anvil sat in the center of it all.

"This is amazing," she murmured. She walked to a spot where an iron gate was propped against a post. The decorative ironwork was so intricate, so artistic that Jordan immediately knew she wasn't in the presence of a craftsman but an artist. She pointed to a huge rosette sitting beside it. "What is this for?"

"That's just a try," he said. "The two I finished were set into the stone wall of a formal garden, kind of like a window."

"I want you," she blurted out, spinning around to face him. "I don't care what it takes, but I want you."

A slow smile curved his lips. "That's always nice to hear."

Jordan groaned inwardly. Never in her life had she been so befuddled by a man. Yes, she found him wildly attractive. What woman wouldn't, him standing there with his shirt unbuttoned to the waist and his gorgeous body tempting her?

But there was something else at work here. He was incredibly talented and impossibly charming and nothing like the men she was usually attracted to. Yet the attraction was undeniable. If he agreed to work for her, she'd have to keep that attraction in check.

Maybe she ought to just walk away. Having him in close proximity was a disaster waiting to happen. What she really needed was a blacksmith who was old and wrinkled and didn't have all his teeth. That kind of man would be so much easier to resist. Danny Quinn was the human equivalent of catnip.

"How much do you want me?" Danny asked.

"What I meant was that I want you to do this job. I can see your talent and I think we can work out a way that your needs—" She cleared her throat. "Your *artistic* needs can be met." Jordan drew a deep breath. "As far as compensation, I'm willing to be generous if you're willing to put all your time and effort into the project until it's finished. Ten-hour days, six days a week if necessary."

"And what kind of compensation are we talking about?"

"Well, it depends on how long you take to finish the job. But I can promise you that it will be very generous. Well worth your while."

"You'll have to include living expenses. I can't work from here."

"Why not?"

"Because I don't want to spend my time making the drive back and forth every time I need to fit something, dragging iron from here to there. We can set up a forge on-site. It will be more efficient. I'll need a place to sleep."

"You don't want to sleep at home?"

"I have to tend the fire and I sometimes work late into the night. I don't need anything posh, just a bed and a shower."

"All right. There's a cottage that you can use."

"And I'm bringing my dogs, too. And I eat three meals a day."

"You expect me to cook for you?" Jordan asked.

"I expect you to feed me," he replied.

The thought of having a man as sexy as Danny around 24/7 was a bit disconcerting. But she was a very capable woman with finely honed self-control. And this was business. Nothing would happen if she didn't want it to happen. "That can all be arranged," she said. "We don't have a cook at the house, but I'll open up an account for you at the market in the village."

"I can live with that." He smiled and a shiver skittered down her spine. "Well, I suppose I ought to see the place, make a few notes and figure out if this is really a job I want to do."

"The sooner the better. I'd like you to start as soon as possible." She paused. "And I should warn you, I'm a very hands-on—" Jordan swallowed hard. In such a highly charged atmosphere, her admission could probably be misconstrued—again. "I meant to say, I'm very concerned with details, so I will be involved in all important decisions."

He cocked his eyebrow, then shrugged. "I have some things to finish up here. Why don't I drive over this evening and you can show me around?"

"That would be fine."

They stood facing each other, an uneasy silence growing between them. Now that their business was completed, Jordan realized she should leave, or risk looking as though she was interested in something more than his blacksmith skills. She held out her hand again. "Well, it was a pleasure meeting you, Mr.—Danny."

He took her fingers in his, his touch so gentle that it was more a caress than a polite gesture. "You have no idea what a pleasure it was for me, Jordan," he murmured.

For a long moment, she wasn't sure what to do. His touch felt so good she didn't want to pull away. Neither one of them took a breath or even blinked, and when he took a step closer, Jordan was certain he was about to kiss her. She yanked her hand back and clutched at the purse slung over her shoulder.

"Later," he said with a crooked smile.

She wasn't sure whether he was referring to their meeting at the castle or his intention to kiss her. "I look forward to it," she stated curtly. "And please don't blow me off this time."

"I wouldn't think of it," he said in a low voice.

Jordan gave him a nod, then strode out of the barn. As soon as she had put a reasonable distance between them, she cursed softly. Had it really been necessary to add that last part? It made her sound like a complete bitch. But from the moment she'd set eyes on Danny Quinn she'd found it impossible to separate pleasure from the business she meant to do with him. She'd have to toughen up if she was going to deal with him—and with the unbidden attraction she felt.

"He's not *that* cute," she said to herself in a feeble attempt to mitigate her feelings. "All right, maybe he *is* really cute. But he's probably just like all gorgeous men—full of himself. And I've always hated men with big egos."

Hopefully, by the time she got back to Castle Cnoc, she'd have convinced herself that Danny was just like all the other workmen wandering about the place—ordinary guys, there to do a job and nothing more.

But as she pulled away from the bakery, she realized it would take a whole lot more than the drive to make that happen.

Maybe a ride to Dublin and back would do it.

DANNY TWISTED THE rearview mirror around to check his appearance. After he'd finished work for the day, he'd grabbed a quick shower and a shave and put on a decent shirt, then set off for Castle Cnoc. He'd thought about walking. Along the coast the castle was not more than an hour's hike. But he didn't want to arrive all sweaty and knackered. For any other girl in County Cork, he wouldn't have bothered to worry. But Jordan Kennally was not just any girl.

She was—well, what the hell was she? he wondered. Sophisticated...and ambitious...and American, three qualities he hadn't really dealt with in his love life to date. No wonder he'd acted like such a fool. Even the best of his pathetic charm had had no effect on her. He'd tried to be cool and he'd sounded like a bleedin' culchie instead. And she'd left acting as though she'd stepped in something with a big stink on it.

"So just keep your gob shut," he muttered. "Smile and nod and let her do all the talking."

He jumped out of the battered Land Rover and slammed the door behind him. He probably should have borrowed Riley's car, just to create a better impression. Hell, he probably should have gone out and bought some new clothes and maybe even stopped for a haircut. And while he was out, he could have bought himself a clue as to how to act around a woman like Jordan.

He stared up at the facade of the old manor. The castle was attached to the huge Georgian house on its north side—the tall stone tower constructed to look out over the surrounding countryside and the sea to the west. Smuggler's Cove was right below the castle, at the bottom of the rocky cliff.

With all the construction around, it was difficult to tell where the front door of the manor house was anymore. Danny wandered over to a scaffold covered in plastic and found the door behind it. He pushed it open and stepped inside the spacious entry hall.

He felt as if he were stepping back in time. His last visit had been during a drunken birthday celebration for one of his schoolmates. At the time, he'd been just shy of eighteen and the manor had been rundown and open to the elements. But now the windowpanes had been replaced with sparkling glass and the crumbling plaster restored to its former beauty. Wainscotting had been polished and floors waxed.

As Jordan had promised, Castle Cnoc's manor house had nearly been restored to its former grandeur.

"Hello?" Danny called.

A soft melody drifted from the rear of the house and he followed the sound, the Irish tune luring him closer.

The imposing dining room at the rear of the ground floor had also been restored, the floor-to-ceiling paneling refinished and shining softly in the late-afternoon sun. A new chandelier hung from the ceiling in the center of the room, crystals twinkling.

The music grew louder as he traced it to the small breakfast room that adjoined the dining room. Danny felt a tiny thrill race through him when he saw her. She was standing on a ladder, her back to him, polishing a stained-glass medallion in one of the leaded windows. A Cara Dillon song played from a small radio.

Jaysus, she was beautiful, tall and slender, but with curves in all the right places. Her dark hair and pale skin made her appear delicate, but Danny already knew better. He suspected that Jordan was the kind of woman who liked to get her own way, and pity any man who wasn't willing to comply. He smiled to himself. Hell, he could stand to be bossed around a bit—especially in the bedroom.

She'd changed out of the turtleneck jumper and jeans that she'd had on earlier and now wore a pretty flowered dress with a green cardie over it. His gaze fixed on her backside and he found himself speculating on the color and style of her knickers.

"White," he murmured to himself. "With lace."

Danny leaned against the doorjamb and continued to watch her, listening to her hum along with the tune. She seemed so relaxed, completely different from the businesslike woman he'd met earlier that morning.

Danny knew it was crazy to want her the way he did.

She was about to become his boss, never mind the fact she'd be leaving Ireland as soon as her work was done at Castle Cnoc. Yet, he couldn't seem to help himself. From the moment he'd set eyes on her, he'd felt a wickedly powerful fascination.

He'd always done his best to avoid lengthy romantic entanglements with women. An occasional one-night stand with an attractive girl was plenty for him. He'd just never been any good at commitment.

His mother had always said it was because he was constantly searching for his muse, the perfect woman who could push his art to greater heights. "Hard work," she'd say, shaking her finger at him. That was the only thing that would bring him true success. But that hadn't stopped him from looking. Still, as he observed Jordan, Danny suspected she was more like one of the enchantresses from the old fairy tales, the *leanan sidhe.* Everything about her was meant to make him ignore reason and surrender to her magic. But the *leanan sidhe* were dangerous. If a man tried to leave such a powerful being he was doomed to death.

Danny slowly walked into the room, taking in the tiny details: the stained glass, the carved rosettes in the dark wood paneling, the decorative plaster medallion on the ceiling. "This is brilliant," he said.

Startled, she clutched at the ladder then glanced over her shoulder. "You scared me! How long have you been standing there?"

"Two verses and a rather lovely chorus." She wobbled on the ladder and he rushed to offer his hand. When he'd captured her fingers in his, Danny grinned. "Look at what you've done to this place. It's a deadly miracle."

"It is?" she said, excitement suffusing her tone. "It's...deadly. Yes. I've been so wrapped up in all the details that sometimes I forget to look at the big picture. It's going to be beautiful when it's all done."

"And you're in charge of all this?"

"Yes. I'm the project manager. The boss." She paused, sending him a suspicious look, then slowly climbed down the ladder. "Is that going to be a problem?"

He held on to her hand, smoothing his fingers over the back of her wrist. "You being in charge? Why would that be a problem?"

"Some men don't like working for women. I've had to fire a handful of them on this project because they wouldn't listen to me. They were...insubordinate. And dismissive. And rude."

"This isn't the type of job that women usually do," Danny said. "But in all honesty, I usually work for the woman of the house so there's no problem that I can see."

She slowly withdrew her hand from his. "Come on, let's go to my office. I've got a lot of the old hardware there and a list of what we need done."

Danny followed her through the dining room and down a narrow hall behind the stairs. She stopped to open a door, but it appeared to be stuck. As Jordan struggled with it, Danny reached around her to help. "Here, let me give it a try."

"No," she insisted. "I can get it." She shoved her shoulder against the door, but it wouldn't budge. "It's as if someone locked it from the inside."

Jordan turned to face him and they found themselves

in an odd embrace, his hands flat against the door on either side of her, trapped in the small alcove of the doorway. He drew a deep breath, the scent of her perfume touching his nose, and leaned closer. A woman didn't wear perfume like that unless she wanted to attract a man.

There was no helping it. Nothing to be done. Without even a second thought, Danny brushed a kiss across her lips. It was a tentative contact and he waited for her response, bracing himself for a slap across the face or a verbal dressing-down.

But to his surprise, Jordan threw her arms around his neck and kissed him back, desperately, hungrily, as if she'd gone without for far too long. At first it was a clumsy kiss, but then Danny took her face between his hands and softly tempered her frenzy with a carefully measured assault.

Almost immediately, she melted against him, her body going limp. A tiny groan slipped from her throat and he drew back and looked down into her flushed face. Her eyes were still closed and he couldn't tell from her expression what she was thinking. Was she embarrassed by her actions? Or well-pleased?

"Jordan?"

She opened her eyes and stared up at him. "Oh, God." The word slipped out of her on a gasp. She twisted out of his embrace and nervously smoothed her hands over her clothes. "That was…unexpected."

He reached out and ran a finger along her flushed cheek. "Now don't get yourself all mortified over it. It was a kiss and nothing more. A very lovely kiss at that," he said.

"Yes." She nodded nervously. "Well, maybe we should just focus on the business at hand."

As far as Danny was concerned, the only business at hand was the business of kissing her again. In truth, he had an entire business plan unfolding in his head. First another kiss, then a caress, and then, maybe full-on seduction. He didn't care a whit about the job, he wanted this woman.

He slipped his hands around her waist and moved her out of the way, then firmly grasped the doorknob. When he turned it and pushed, the door easily swung open. He chuckled softly. "Clever," he said. "If you wanted me to kiss you, you should have just asked."

"It was locked!" Jordan cried.

"And now, it's unlocked."

Jordan gave him an odd look. "I wasn't trying to get you to kiss me," she said, walking past him into the library. "These things happen around here all the time. Doors are locked, then they aren't. Windows are closed, then they aren't. Things go missing and then they turn up a day later."

"Sounds like brownies," Danny said. "Or leprechauns."

"Don't be ridiculous."

"Or ghosts. Or fairies. We have all manner of fantastical creatures here in Ireland. And none of them up to any good at all."

"I don't believe in any of those things," Jordan said.

Danny followed her into the library, making a careful study of the backside of her beautiful body. He fought the urge to slip his arms around her again and pull her into another kiss. Instead, he distracted himself with exploring the interior of the old library.

A memory flashed in his mind and he chuckled softly. "I do remember this room," he murmured. "I lost something here."

"Well, I don't think you'll find it after all these years," Jordan said. "But you're welcome to look."

"I don't think I'd want to find it," he said. "She was seventeen and I was fifteen. And I thought I knew everything about girls. After that night, I realized I knew nothing."

"You mean you—"

Danny nodded. "I lost my virginity right about—" he stepped to a spot in front of the fireplace "—here, I believe. I was drunk on whiskey and she was looking for a bit of fun. The minute she put her hands on me, I knew the world would never be the same."

"Right here?"

Danny nodded. "God, that seems like just yesterday."

"How old are you?" she asked.

"Twenty-six. How old are you?"

She tipped her chin up and, for a moment, he thought he'd insulted her. "Twenty-seven."

He grinned. "I've always gone for older girls." Danny continued his stroll around the room. Instead of books, the shelves were filled with pieces of decorative plaster and wood carvings, doorknobs and ceramic tile, and an entire wall of iron hardware.

"We've collected samples of all the hardware that needs to be replicated," she said. "It's on these two bottom shelves." Jordan turned and searched the cluttered surface of the desk, then glanced nervously over her shoulder.

"What's wrong?" Danny asked.

"Nothing," she murmured with a frown. "I just misplaced something."

"I can help you look," he said. "What is it?"

"No," she said. "It's probably gone."

Danny walked over to the desk. "What was it?"

"An old door knocker, made of cast iron. It was really beautiful. I found it half-buried in the garden. I was hoping that we could make them for all the exterior doors." She sighed, shaking her head as she braced her hands on her hips. "I don't know who's been in here, but I'm about to put in a surveillance system to find out."

"Leprechauns steal things from houses. Brownies like to live with humans and torment them for amusement."

"I told you, I don't believe in leprechauns or brownies."

"You should. You're in Ireland," he teased. "You've got to let the country into your bones. After all, with a name like Kennally, I'd wager you have a drop or two of Irish blood in you."

Jordan laughed softly. "I'm a quarter Irish. My father's father." She shook her head. "I probably just misplaced it. It'll turn up later." She picked up a paper from her desk and held it out to him. "Here's the inventory of what we need. They're numbered to correspond with the samples on the shelf." She opened her mouth, then snapped it shut again.

Danny gave her a curious look. "Was there something else?"

"About what just happened outside in the hallway. I want you to know that that kind of behavior is absolutely inappropriate and I'm sorry that I let my—my—Whatever. I'm just sorry. And it will never, ever happen again."

"Jaysus, don't say that. It's really the only thing that makes me want to take this job," Danny admitted. "Replicating hinges isn't nearly as exciting as kissing you."

"But we can't," she insisted.

"Why not?" He backed her up against the edge of the desk and braced his hands beside her hips. Once again, he met no resistance when he kissed her. If anything, she seemed to enjoy it even more this time. He took care to make the kiss deliciously tantalizing, invading her mouth with his tongue.

"See," he whispered against her lips. "It's very simple. I lean forward and you lean forward and it happens."

"We can't," she said again.

"Yes, we can," he said. "Forget the job. I don't need the job if that's what's standing in the way."

"But I need you to do the job," she insisted. "Much more than I need you to do...this. We need to keep it strictly business."

"I don't do business," he said. "It's art. There are no rules. And I refuse to consider you my boss. You can, however, be my muse."

A smile quirked at the corners of her mouth. "I'll be a muse for hinges and gates?"

Danny nodded. "I'll need one. The job itself promises to be a bit of a snore."

"Mr. Quinn, you are completely full of shite."

He stepped back as she fixed him with an irritated glare. "I see you've picked up the language, if not the mythology," he said. Sure, he'd pulled the last straight out of his arse, but right now, he'd say just about anything to get her to kiss him again.

"Will you do the job?"

"Are you going to let me kiss you again?"

She shook her head. "This project is very important to me, Mr. Quinn."

"If you call me Mr. Quinn again, I'll walk out of here and you can get Neddy O'Doul to do your work. He usually shoes horses and he makes a hames of that."

"Danny," she said. "My future depends upon this project. It has to come in on time and under budget. You have no idea how much is riding on this. We can't have any distractions."

He wasn't going to get any closer to Jordan sitting at home. He'd have to take the bad with the good. "I'll do the job," he said. "You won't have to worry." He pushed away from the desk and saw relief flood her features. All the tension in her body eased. "Tell me why this is so important."

"I have a lot to prove to my boss, who just happens to be my father. If I do a good job here, then maybe he'll finally recognize that I'm competent and trustworthy. And as good as any son he has."

"You work for your father?"

"Yes. I've worked for his real estate development and construction firm since I was in high school. Some day, I plan to run it." Jordan paused, then smiled weakly. "I'll just have to find a way to get rid of my four older brothers first, but I'm working on that."

"Well, I'll have to make sure that you get what you want while you're here," Danny said.

She nodded. "Yes. Fine. I suppose we should talk about compensation."

"I don't like to talk about money," he said. "That's business. And it will be difficult to know how much this will cost until I buy materials and get started."

"But I have to have some idea," she said, concern furrowing her brow.

"What's your budget?"

"Thirty thousand plus materials," she stated.

"Materials. There's where the budget could go to hell. You'll have to decide if you want iron or steel."

"What's the difference?"

"Iron is authentic to the time period but very expensive. Steel is cheaper, but it doesn't have the same look."

"Iron," she said. "When aesthetics make a difference. Steel, when practicality is important. This has to be an authentic restoration."

"The labor budget sounds more than reasonable," he said. In truth, it was enough to live on for a good year. Once he completed this job, he could spend the next twelve months working on his art instead of working in the smithy. "You've got your man."

She relaxed and smiled. "Good."

"Now, why don't you show me where I'm going to live and where I'll set up the forge."

They made a quick tour of the house, upstairs and down, then walked outside to tour the collection of stone buildings that surrounded the manor. There was a stable, a barn and a huge garden with a newly restored drystone wall. "You'll need a gate for this?" he asked, peering over.

An elderly man and woman were inside, wearing wide-brimmed hats and wellies, standing among huge piles of earth. They stared down into a hole in the ground, not noticing Danny and Jordan. "What are they doing?" he asked.

"That's Bartie and his friend, Daisy. They run the garden club in Glencairn. They showed up one morning and volunteered to do the work for free if I paid for the plantings. Bartie claims that he played in the garden as a child."

"Folks around the county weren't very happy to hear that an American bought this place," he said. "They're kind of suspicious of outsiders."

"I know. But I'm employing a lot of local craftsmen and once they find out who bought the place, they'll be fine. The person is of Irish descent. In fact, she can trace her family back to the original builders of the castle."

"Are you going to tell me who it is, then?"

"You have to promise not to say anything. Until she moves in, she'd like to avoid publicity."

Jordan leaned forward and whispered a familiar name into his ear. There weren't many actors living in County Cork, and now they were about to gain a certified American movie star. "Holy Mary, now there's some news."

She pressed her finger to her lips and shook her head. "Don't tell."

He pressed his own finger to his lips. "Silent as the grave, I'll be." Danny glanced back inside the garden. "So, what are they doing in there?"

"Some Irish thing. Purifying the soil, I believe he calls it. Something about the peat and the sea air and leachings from limestone. I don't really understand it. But he promises I'll have a beautiful rose garden in the end."

"Where do I stay?" Danny asked. "And where do I set up the forge?"

Jordan pointed down the path as they continued on. "There's an old laundry cottage back there with an existing hearth. I think that will do for the forge. And there's the cottage you can use for your living quarters. It was the first place we renovated," Jordan explained. "I used it as my home and office until the manor house had a decent roof and plumbing. It's very comfortable."

She unlocked the door and walked inside. Danny followed her to find a cozy place not much different from his cottage in Ballykirk, a bedroom on one end and a kitchen and bath on the other, with a large living area in between.

"I hope it's all right." Jordan motioned to the bedroom. "The bed is brand-new. There's electric heat and a shower in the bathroom. And a functioning kitchen."

"This will be fine," he said. "I can start moving in tomorrow."

"Good," she murmured.

He reached out and took her hand in his, weaving their fingers together. "So, I guess that would be it, Miss Kennally. Everything is settled between us?"

"Yes," she said, watching him play with her hand. "I—I look forward to working with you, Mr.—I mean, Daniel. Danny. Dan?"

"Danny," he said. He took her hand and turned it

over, then placed her palm on his chest, covering her hand with his. He wanted to do so much more. "I would kiss you, but now that we've come to an agreement, we'll have plenty of time for that later."

"Well, you got what you wanted," she said. "And I got exactly what I wanted. That's what makes a good business deal, don't you think?"

"I got the first thing I wanted. But there's always room for renegotiation." With that, he let her hand drop and turned to the door of the cottage. It took all his will-power to walk away. "I'll see you tomorrow, Jordan."

He left her standing in the center of the room, her green eyes wide, her lips parted. As Danny strode back to his car, he couldn't help but wonder if all that had happened between them had simply been a way to secure his services. When she'd come to the smithy that morning, she'd been determined to convince him to work for her and here he was, ready to drop every-thing and move into her caretaker's cottage.

No, Danny thought to himself. He knew how to read women and she was just as attracted to him as he was to her. There was a lot about this job he was going to like, Danny mused. And spending more time with Jordan Kennally was top on the list.

2

JORDAN ROLLED OVER in bed and stared at the alarm clock on the bedside table. It was almost 8:00 a.m. and she'd only managed a few hours of sleep. She was always up early, supervising the workmen, putting together the daily schedule, checking on supplies and invoices. This morning, she'd risen at sunrise, unlocked the doors, then crawled back into bed.

After what had happened yesterday with Danny Quinn, her whole routine had been thrown into a tailspin. Now, all she could think about was the way he'd kissed her and touched her, the feel of his chest beneath her palms, the way he seemed to ignite her desire with just one look.

Jordan groaned and pulled the pillow over her head. "I've been in Ireland too long," she murmured. "I need to get back to my real life in New York."

But she knew she was only kidding herself. The longer she'd stayed in Ireland, the more she'd grown to enjoy the feelings of freedom. Here she didn't have to worry about pleasing her father or competing with her brothers or avoiding her mother's endless attempts at matchmaking. Here, she did her job and she enjoyed it.

That had been easy until now. She hadn't had any trouble keeping her mind on business. But after her encounter with Danny, maybe the effort had finally become too much to handle. The stress of devoting her every waking moment to this project had finally made her crack.

Never, ever, in her life had she thrown herself at a guy the way she had with him. He was, admittedly, the most handsome man she'd ever met. That dark hair and those incredible blue eyes. And that smile that sent shivers racing through her body. Undeniable lust was only a natural reaction.

But it was more than that. It felt good to be wanted. She'd spent so much time trying to make her way in the men's club that was Kencor that she'd almost forgotten she was a woman. Danny had reminded her that she was pretty and interesting and maybe even a little sexy.

He was a charming bloke, as the Irish would say. Talented, too. She'd always admired artistic people. Though she'd possessed a knack for design, she'd majored in business in college. And her eye for choosing fabrics and furniture wasn't nearly as interesting as that of a painter or sculptor.

But this project would be done in less than three months and she'd be ready to move on to something bigger and better at Kencor. Her father was in negotiation to buy an old Manhattan hotel and she wanted that project more than anything. She wasn't about to allow

herself to be distracted by a man—even one as sexy
as Danny.

Jordan had sought her father's approval from the time
she knew what it was. But he'd never really noticed her,
devoting his attention to his four sons. In truth, Jordan
had always felt that she'd been born to satisfy her mother's need for a daughter.

She'd spent her entire life trying to hide the fact
that she was a girl. As a child, she'd dressed just like
her brothers, in jeans and T-shirts, trying desperately
to keep up with them in every activity from football
to fishing. As a teen, she'd turned her competitiveness
toward her education, refusing to take anything but the
honors courses that her brothers had completed before
her. And though she'd longed to major in interior design
in college, she'd chosen business instead, like her brothers.

This was the project that would finally prove she was
just as competent as any son Andrew Kennally had.
He'd tossed this project to her, deeming it a good job
for a girl. The fact that it was in Ireland made it even
better. It would get Jordan out of the way for a year or
two. But she'd determined that Castle Cnoc would prove
her worthy of so much more.

Jordan snuggled back beneath the covers. If she could
just catch a few more hours, she'd be ready to deal with
the arrival of her new blacksmith. "Danny," she murmured. "Danny Quinn." She closed her eyes and an
image of the handsome Irishman swirled around in her
head.

It wasn't wrong to indulge her attraction in private.
Though sleeping with an employee was against every

code she followed, sleeping with the fantasy of him was perfectly acceptable—as long as she didn't tell anyone.

The sound of barking dogs invaded her waking dream and she brushed it aside. But then she heard a car door slam and that brought Jordan upright in bed. Tossing the covers aside, she raced over to the window that overlooked the front drive.

Two very familiar dogs ran around Danny's battered Land Rover. "Oh, shit!" she muttered, running her hands through her tangled hair. How was it possible that he was here already? Had he stayed up all night packing? Somehow, she couldn't imagine a man like Danny being so excited about moving in that he couldn't sleep through the night. No, only silly, infatuated, desperate women did that.

Jordan scrambled to get dressed, pulling on a pair of jeans and a T-shirt, with no time for underwear. As she slipped on a pair of loafers, she ran her hands through her tangled hair. Today she'd regain her footing with this man. She'd act professionally and she wouldn't let anything he said or did tempt her. Time to get back to business. "Stay strong, be firm," she murmured to herself.

Jordan grabbed her sweater, then raced down the stairs and ran though the entrance hall. Opening the plywood front door, she expected to find Danny waiting on the other side, but he wasn't. She walked beneath the scaffolding and pushed the plastic aside to find him sitting on the tailgate of his Land Rover, staring up at the facade of the manor house as he chatted with Bartie the gardener.

The dogs saw her first and they came trotting up.

"Hi, puppies," she mumbled. What were their names? Mogue was one. "Finny," she said. "Finny and Mogue."

"They seem excited to move in," Danny commented.

She glanced up at him, blinking against the morning light. "I'd prefer that they didn't come in the main house," she said.

"No problems," he said. "They sleep with me."

Another image of him flashed in her head, naked, lying in her bed, the covers tossed aside. What did he mean by that? Had he decided he wasn't interested in sharing her bed? Jordan closed her eyes and banished the erotic fantasy from her head. "Morning, Bartie. You're here early." She glanced down to find the old man holding what looked like a metal detector. "What's that?"

"Special thing it is. Got it from a gardener friend of mine. Supposed to measure the ferrous metals in the soil. Ferrous metals. Very bad for roses, I'm afraid."

"Yes, well. Good luck with that. You're not paying rental for it, are you?"

"No, no. 'Tis a loan." Bartie nodded at them both, then strode off around the side of the manor house, his pace sprightly for a man of his years.

"Ferrous metals?" Danny asked. "What are those?"

Jordan shrugged. "I have no idea. Something Irish I suspect. According to Bartie, it's a wonder anything grows in Ireland."

"My mother has a beautiful rose garden at our family cottage," Danny said. "I never heard her complain about..."

"Ferrous metals," Jordan said. She held her hand up

to the sun, squinting at him. "I was just going to make a pot of coffee. Would you like some?"

He pushed up from his seat on the tailgate. "Actually, I'm going to start unpacking my things. My brother Riley is going to bring my anvil and tools. And I've set up a coal delivery for today. Steel is coming in tomorrow. Can I drive around to the back?"

"Of course," she said. "Well, it seems as if you have things under control."

He chuckled softly, shoving his hands in the back pockets of his jeans. "Appearances can be deceiving. Right now, all I can think about is kissing you again. I'd say control is the last thing on my mind."

"The hours from eight until five are considered work hours," she said. "With an hour for lunch." But though her warning effectively shut him up, Jordan was secretly pleased he was still thinking of her as a woman rather than a boss. Maybe they could stretch the rules a bit. A kiss here and there couldn't hurt, could it?

"After I get some coffee, I'll come and help you unload." She groaned inwardly at her choice of words. Everything she said to him sounded sexual now.

"Bring me a cup and I'll meet you there," he said.

She nodded. "Fine. I'll come in just a—" This was ridiculous! "I'll be just a moment." Jordan turned on her heel and walked back inside the manor. When she reached the safety of the kitchen, she clapped her hands to her warm cheeks. "Get a grip," she muttered to herself. At this rate, they'd be in bed by lunchtime and exploring their deepest sexual fantasies by dinner.

If this was the way it was going to be every day that he was here, she wondered how she'd survive. Her heart was beating double-time and her nerves were so jangled she wanted to scream at the top of her lungs.

The coffeemaker had been set up the night before and Jordan simply pushed a button and waited as the glass pot began to fill. Sitting at the huge worktable in the center of the kitchen, she cupped her chin in her palm and considered the men she'd allowed into her life—and into her bed.

Though she'd had a number of lovers in the past, none of them had really moved her. The relationships had always been enjoyable, the sex interesting, but she'd always held something back. And Jordan was self-aware enough to put the blame for this on her relationship with her father.

Though she'd struggled to win his approval, she sometimes resented the control he held over her life. Andrew Kennally could snap his fingers any time of the day or night and she'd come running, ready to do his bidding. But she had refused to do the same for any man in her life. And in the end, they'd never wanted to compete with a man as powerful as Andrew Kennally.

Jordan wondered what it would be like to let go of all the baggage she carried around. Just to set it down and feel completely at ease for once. What harm could a little romantic fling do? There were few people around to witness any dalliance, just a workman here and there. Bartie and Daisy were too preoccupied with the garden to pay any notice. And everyone left at five, giving her all evening alone with Danny on this remote seaside estate.

The coffeemaker clicked off, startling her back to reality. It was a risk, pure and simple. If her father found out, he'd be furious. Sex with an employee was forbidden by company policy. She could be sued for sexual harassment, putting her entire professional future at Kencor in jeopardy.

Jordan grabbed a pair of mugs from a nearby cupboard and filled them, then put sugar and creamer in one and left the other black. After this morning, she'd know exactly how he liked his coffee. And by the end of the day, Jordan was certain she'd know a lot of other things about Danny.

Anticipation mixed with fear as she walked out the kitchen door and toward the caretaker's cottage. The dogs were romping along the garden path and joined her, trotting along behind. "I don't want the two of you digging up any of the new plantings in the garden," she ordered. "And if you have to poop, run out along the cliff to do it."

Finny and Mogue looked up at her as if they understood everything she was saying. But she made a mental note to repeat the rules to their owner as well.

When she reached the cottage, she found Danny inside, his belongings tossed in the middle of the living area. He emerged a few moments later from the kitchen, his canvas jacket gone. He wore a faded T-shirt that hugged the muscles of his chest and dangled loosely around his waist.

"There's beer in the fridge," he said.

"I stocked the refrigerator last night." She frowned. "Do you drink your beer warm?"

He crossed the room to stand in front of her. "No. Cold is fine. And I drink my coffee hot and black." She handed him the proper mug. "That was nice of you. Very thoughtful…for a boss."

She knew immediately that he was teasing. There was a definitely a twinkle in his eye and a devilish smile playing across his lips. "I just wanted to make sure you were comfortable," Jordan said.

"I have drink. What about food?"

"You're on your own there," she said. "I set up the account for you at the market. They'll have everything you need to make meals."

"You're not going to cook for me?" He put on a pout. "I thought that was part of the deal."

"No, I think I made it quite clear yesterday that I don't cook."

"Ah, but I do," he said. "Good thing."

Jordan had been surviving on sandwiches and cereal for most of her stay. A few nights a week, she went into town and had a decent dinner at one of the pubs there. But she'd longed to explore a bit further. She just needed a dinner partner. "I'll pay for dinners out whenever you care to go," she said.

"If you come along, it's a deal."

Danny rested his hand on her hip. Jordan's breath caught in her throat. Were they at that point already, that he could touch her without even having a good reason?

"It's a deal," she repeated.

"I'm gummin' for a decent breakfast. Why don't I finish unpacking and we'll go out and get something. My treat."

Jordan was tempted by his offer. She usually didn't leave the worksite during the day. But the men who were scheduled knew their jobs and would keep an eye on the house. "All right," she said. "Let me just make a few phone calls."

"Fifteen minutes?" he asked.

"Yes. I'll be back."

The minute Jordan got out of the cottage, she ran. Back to the manor house, up the stairs and into her room. Fifteen minutes was just enough time for a shower. She hadn't shaved her legs in a week, but that would have to wait. Though it was just a simple breakfast, Jordan couldn't help but be excited. Any excuse to spend time with Danny was worth celebrating.

"TELL ME ALL ABOUT YOURSELF," Danny asked, staring at Jordan over the rim of his coffee cup. "And spare no details."

There was no doubt about it. He found her endlessly fascinating and they didn't even know each other yet. He watched as she spread jam on her toast in a precise manner, then took a tiny bite out of it. It wasn't just her body, he mused, although that was just grand. He found himself caught up in the chase, the desire to possess a woman who was equally determined to avoid him.

Sure, they'd shared a few kisses, but according to Jordan, it would have to end there. But that wouldn't stop him from trying. He wanted to know what she looked like naked, how her body felt beneath his hands, what she talked about in her sleep. But even that wasn't enough. He wanted to know about her life, the people she loved, her dreams, her fears.

Danny had usually satisfied himself with the superficial and left it at that. But there was something about

Jordan that made him want to know more. Was it just curiosity or was there some deeper connection?

"Are you going to eat that toast or paint a portrait of the Mona Lisa with raspberry jam?" He grabbed her hand and took a bite, then grinned.

"Hey! Eat your own toast."

"I like yours better," he said. Though she did everything to perfection, from buttering toast to renovating the manor house, there was one thing that seemed to escape her—flirting.

"What do you want to know?" she asked.

"Tell me about your family," he ordered.

"Only if you tell me about yours," she countered.

"Agreed. You first."

"All right. There's not much to tell. I have four older brothers who work for the family business. My father thinks I should decorate houses but I think I should get the same chance to run Kencor as my brothers have. So I work as hard as I can."

"You and your father don't get on?" Danny asked.

Jordan shook her head. "I'm sure he loves me just as any father would. But he doesn't really trust me. I think I remind him of my mother. She drives him crazy." She took a bite of her eggs. "I suppose you have a normal family life?"

"As normal as it gets," Danny replied. "Two sisters, two brothers, all older. I know what it's like to be on the trailing end. I was always following my brothers around. My folks own a pub in Ballykirk. The Speckled Hound. My sisters are both married, both teachers. You know Kell. He's the oldest boy and then there's Riley. He's a musician and he helps my folks with the pub."

"And how did you become a blacksmith?" she asked.

"I went to art school and studied sculpting and along the way I started working in metal. It was the next logical step. I saw a demonstration at one of the heritage festivals and went to a few workshops. Then I spent my summer holiday working for a smith up in Galway."

"It seems like such hard work to make that iron do what you want it to."

"It is. It's a slow process. It gives you time to think and plan and visualize what you want it to be. All the architectural stuff is just to pay the bills. Someday, I'd like to focus entirely on sculpture."

"I saw the work in your portfolio. The willow tree that you did, the one that was blowing in the wind, that was one of the most beautiful things I've ever seen. I want it for the garden here."

"You'll have to steal it from the lady I sold it to in Dublin," he said. "It's sitting in the lobby of her posh hotel."

"You should show in a gallery," she said.

"I have a few things in a show opening next month. And I've had my own show a few times at a gallery one of my friends runs." He paused, observing her from across the table. "What about a boyfriend?"

His question took her by surprise and Danny cursed inwardly, knowing he should have waited. But there was no reason not to be honest about his interest in her.

"Sorry," he said. "Just curious."

"You first," Jordan countered. "Do you have a girl-friend? Or do you have five or six?"

"I have no girlfriend," he said. "There was someone about a year ago, for about a month, but that ended. No hard feelings. Most women are looking for a little bit better than I'm able to provide. Now you."

"There is a guy I used to see in New York. But we were never in a committed relationship. We were just…" She cleared her throat. "Friends."

"You're just dating then?"

"Well, no." She frowned. "Yes. At least I was. I'm sure we'll see each other again when I get back to New York."

"Naked?" he asked.

She gasped. "What?"

"Will you see each other naked? It's a simple question."

"That's none of your business," she replied.

"Well, it is. I don't want to cause any problems between you and your man."

"He's not my man. I don't have a man," Jordan said. "I'm single and that's all I have to say about it."

"You sound a wee bit prickly there," he said. "Did I touch on a sore subject?"

"You're awfully nosy for someone I've just met."

"Curious," he said. "That's a better word for it. So, now it's your turn. Ask me anything you like. Anything at all."

He picked up a slice of bacon and bit off the end, then waited for her to come up with an appropriate question. But she seemed to struggle. "You want to know whether I can be discreet," he finally said. "You want to know that, if we indulge, it won't blow up in your face. And you really want to know what I look like naked."

A nervous laugh burst from her lips. "No," she said, shaking her head.

"Yes," Danny countered, reaching across the table to capture her hand. "You do." He opened her fingers and placed a kiss on her palm. "I look feckin' fabulous, just to let you know."

Jordan gasped, pulling her hand away. "Are you always so bold?"

"Absolutely."

A pretty blush stained her cheeks. "I'll take your word for it."

"And I can be discreet, too," he said.

"I don't need complications," Jordan murmured.

"It's very simple, then. Whenever we're alone, I have permission to kiss you. And we'll see where it leads? Sound good?"

"It sounds very good. I'm just not—"

He reached out and pressed his finger to her lips. "Leave it at that," he said. "Talking about it isn't nearly as much fun as doing it." He picked up a piece of toast from his plate and held it out to her. "Can you put some jam on this?"

Jordan stared at the toast. "What?"

"I like the way you do it. You spread it out right to the edge. Perfectly perfect without any drips."

"Are you making fun of me?" she asked.

"A little bit. But I fancy what I see."

"And in between all this kissing, you're going to get your work done?"

"That's what I'm here for," he said. "I thought I'd start with the big projects first and cross them off the list and—"

"No," Jordan interrupted. "No, we have to have the

hinges first. The doors will be back next week and they all have to be hung. The hardware comes first."

"All right," he said, nodding. "Hardware first."

"I have it all laid out on a spreadsheet," she explained. "And a flowchart. I can show them to you if you'd like. I'll make you a copy."

"No need," Danny said. "I'm sure I can get along without." He smiled at her. "I like a woman who takes charge."

"All right. I'm a little obsessive-compulsive. But that's not a bad thing. I wouldn't have gotten where I am if I didn't care about details."

"You've been in Ireland for how long?"

"Sixteen months," she said. "But for the first year I went back and forth to New York once a month."

"You've spent too much time shut up in that house. We're going to have to loosen you up, woman. Show you what Ireland is really like. I'll wager you'll become so fond of the place, you'll never want to leave."

"And how do you propose to do that?"

"I have my ways," he said.

The rest of the breakfast passed in lighthearted conversation. He learned more about the project and about Jordan. Though she spent most of her free time working, it wasn't for lack of interest in the surrounding countryside. She'd visited many of the estates open to the public and spent time at museums and shops in Dublin, Galway and Cork. But she'd never been out to a pub on a Saturday night.

They'd have two, maybe three months together. If he couldn't provide her with a bit of fun and excitement in that time, then he didn't deserve to be called an Irishman. "So what do you do for fun if you're not out at the pubs?" he asked. "When you need a break or you want to relax, what do you do?

She gave him an odd look. "I have fun."

"How?" he said.

Jordan seemed reluctant to tell him. "I read, I listen to music."

"That sounds like fun," he said, grinning.

"And now I'm looking for the brownies that keep stealing things from the house," she said.

"You believe in brownies now?"

"I don't know what to believe. But things disappear in the middle of night. I found an old ring in one of the bathrooms. I set it on the sink and a day later, it was gone. Then it turned up in the bottom of a cabinet."

"Hmm. I suppose I could spend the night with you and we'd search out those brownies soon enough," Danny suggested.

Jordan met his gaze. "You're a nice guy, Daniel Quinn. But we won't be sleeping together."

"You don't even know me yet," Danny teased. "If you did, you'd realize that I'm far from nice. In fact, I'm very, very naughty. As for sleeping together, it's a little soon to be makin' a statement like that, don't you think?"

BY THE END OF THE DAY, Danny had managed to get the old laundry set up as a temporary forge. It had been impossible for Jordan to get any work done and she found herself standing at the second-story windows and staring out over the garden, hoping to catch a glimpse of him in the yard beyond.

By the third visit, when she'd brought him a glass of lemonade and a ham sandwich, he'd finished hanging all his tools from a chain stretched across the old laundry.

The coal was delivered by truck after lunch, and she stood and chatted with him as he filled a wheelbarrow full and dumped it beside the hearth. It was almost too much to bear, watching the play of muscle beneath his smooth skin as he worked. She wanted to reach out and run her hands over his shoulders and down his back; but she was left to pretend that his shirtless state had no effect on her at all.

She was thankful that the two dogs were a constant presence; when she ran out of things to say, she'd toss them a stick or rub their bellies.

The sun was beginning to descend in the west when Jordan decided to ask about Danny's plans for dinner. She'd promised to provide him with a decent meal and she couldn't think of anything else that might provide them with more time together.

She grabbed the bag of dog treats she'd purchased in the village that afternoon and headed out to the temporary smithy. Finny and Mogue were asleep in the doorway and she called to them, then tossed a treat up in the air. To her surprise, Finny leapt and caught it in mid-flight. When she tossed one Mogue's way, Finny cut the smaller dog off and grabbed a second bite. "Don't be so greedy," she cried. "You've already had one."

"You're spoiling them," Danny called from the doorway.

Jordan glanced up, then straightened. Every time she saw him, a tiny thrill raced through her. She wondered when they'd kiss again. "I like them," she said. "We always had dogs when I was young. Golden retrievers, mostly."

"Why not get one now?"

"With my schedule? I wouldn't have time to spend with a pet. It wouldn't be fair."

"Well, you can have these two for as long as I stay. If you keep feeding them treats, they won't listen to me anyway."

She closed the bag. "So, how are things going?"

"I'm ready to start. Iron and steel stock is coming tomorrow. I've finished patterns for the hinges and I should be able to start work on those as soon as I get materials. Here, let me show you."

She followed him inside to a scarred wooden table he'd found in the stable. "I've looked at the doors and they weigh a ton. I'd recommend that you use modern-day hinges for strength. They'll last longer, they'll operate more smoothly and I can make dummy straps, so they'll look like the originals."

"If you think that's best," she said. "I'll trust your judgment."

"I think that's best," he said. "And it will save you some money."

"Good. I like that." Her gaze scanned his naked torso. "Are you finished for the day?"

He nodded. "I was just going to take a quick shower."

"Come with me. I want to show you something."

"It's past five," he said. "I'm knackered."

She reached out and grabbed his hand. "This isn't work. You'll like it. I promise."

She pulled him outside, reveling in the feel of his

fingers laced through hers. Just the simple act of touching him was enough to send a surge of need through her. She wondered what it might be like to be able to touch him at will, to have the complete freedom to explore his body.

They walked through the house and then down a narrow hallway behind the butler's pantry. Jordan opened a door and flipped on a light switch before leading him down a short flight of stairs. The air was moist and a familiar scent teased at her nose.

She flipped another switch and the lights illuminated a huge room with an arched ceiling. Set below them was a swimming pool, the underwater lights creating strange shadows on the walls.

Danny gasped. "Jaysus, has this been here all along?"

Jordan nodded. "The water was drained, of course, and it was full of musty old wicker furniture when I got here. And all the plumbing was rusted, but it's all functioning now." She stared up at the ceiling. "The tiles were hand-painted by an artist in Belfast. And they were installed by workmen who worked on the *Titanic.* Luckily, they were in perfect condition. Replacing them would have been ridiculously expensive."

Danny stared up at the ceiling. "Half-naked fairies must have been pretty racy for the turn of the century."

"I'm sure they were," Jordan said. "There are mermaids beneath the water."

"You shouldn't have brought me here," Danny said, shifting his gaze to the water. "It's like holding out a bottle of water to a man dying of thirst."

"You want to swim? Go ahead. It took forever to fill.

Nearly a week, but the new heater is working and it's warm enough to use now."

"Really?" Danny didn't wait for her answer. He tugged off his T-shirt as he kicked off his shoes and socks. But when he reached for the button on his jeans, Jordan sucked in a sharp breath. Danny glanced up and she quickly tried to compose herself. "Sorry. I figured boxers were just as good as a bathing suit."

"Oh, no," she said, "that's fine. Go right ahead."

"Turn around," he said, twirling his finger in the air. "I wouldn't want to make you blush. Unless, that was your plan all along in bringing me here. Getting me starkers."

"That's exactly what I was thinking of," Jordan said. "Go ahead, what are you waiting for? I'm looking forward to the superhero underwear."

He glanced down then winced. "To tell the truth, I seem to have forgotten my underwear this morning," he replied.

She quickly covered her eyes and a moment later, she heard him jump into the shallow end of the pool. When she looked again he was submerged and swimming to the deep end, his naked form visible beneath the wavering water. As he came closer to the surface, she turned back around.

"All right," he called. "You can look now."

She peered through her fingers. Danny bobbed at the far end of the pool, his arms stretched out along the tile deck. "Are you going to come in? The water's beautiful. Warm enough to be comfortable, cool enough to be refreshing."

"You're naked," she said.

"I promise, I'll stay on this end. And if you're shy, just leave your clothes on."

"I'm not going to jump in with my clothes on."

"Then take your clothes off. I won't look." Danny watched her face as she considered her options. "Oh, I can see those wheels turning. Should I cast aside my inhibitions and give it a go? Or should I pretend like I'm a good girl? I know you're not a good girl, Jordan. There's a wild woman under that proper dress and cardie."

"Don't presume to know what I'm thinking," she warned.

"We're both adults," he said.

"I'm your boss, you're my employee."

"I'm your artist, you're my muse," he countered.

"More like I'm a canary and you're a hungry cat," she said.

"All right, don't come in." He pushed off the side and submerged, kicking and stroking beneath the water before he came up in the middle of the pool. "This is incredible. The perfect way to relax after a long day at work. A bloke could get used to living like this. In the lap of luxury."

"Money doesn't always buy happiness," Jordan said.

"Who says that? And who even believes that's true?"

"I do," she said. Jordan kicked off her shoes and pulled up her skirt, then sat down on the edge of the pool, dangling her feet in the water. "My father has all the money in the world and he's never really been happy. He always seems to need more. When is it finally enough? When can you sit back and enjoy what you have?"

"I don't know," Danny said. "I never really thought about it."

"I do," she said. "All the time."

"Are you happy?" he asked. "I mean, right now, at this moment." She thought about her answer for a long moment, a frown wrinkling her brow. "It's not a trick question."

"It's not the money. That's not why I want a place at Kencor. I'd work for free if it were challenging work. I love my job."

He swam across the pool and stood in front of her, the water lapping at his waist. Droplets streamed over his skin and clung to his lashes. "You don't convince me," he said softly. "I want to know what makes you smile."

"Watching silly animal videos on YouTube," she said. "Eating a whole pint of chocolate ice cream at three in the morning. Getting the hiccups from drinking too much champagne."

"Do I make you smile?" he asked. Danny wrapped his arms around her legs and gently pulled her closer to the edge. "When I touch you?" He smoothed his hand along her thigh, beneath her skirt. "Would you smile if I dragged you in?"

"No," she warned. "I'd be mad. My phone is in my pocket and I don't think my watch is waterproof."

Danny stepped between her knees and reached up to slip his hand around her nape. He gently pulled her toward him until their lips were just a few inches apart.

A tiny sigh slipped from her throat when he removed her watch from her wrist and set it on the pool deck. Then, Danny smoothed his hands over the skirt of her dress until he found her cell phone. He slipped it out of her pocket and set it beside her watch, then gently pulled her into the water. Jordan didn't even bother to protest. What was the point? Trying to deny her impulses would only frustrate them both.

When her feet touched bottom, she reached for the hem of her dress and pulled it over her head, then tossed it to the pool deck. She'd chosen her underwear very carefully that morning and was satisfied that the scraps of lace and satin were enough for now.

Though it was difficult to ignore the fact that Danny was naked, Jordan decided to keep her gaze fixed firmly on his face to avoid any embarrassing moments. "It *is* nice," she said.

He slipped his hands around her waist, his attention moving to her lips. "I'm going to kiss you again," he murmured. "It's past five, so I think it's legal."

He leaned forward and brushed his damp lips against hers. A flood of need raced through her and suddenly, she felt as if her heart might beat right out of her chest.

Maybe it was the warm water or their lack of clothing, but any attempt at self-control by either one of them had gone missing. Her fingers furrowed through his hair as the kiss deepened. She couldn't breathe, couldn't think. Every ounce of her being was focusing on the wild sensations racing through her body.

She wanted to stop, or at least slow down, but she seemed unable to put together the will. When his lips trailed along her shoulder, Jordan gasped. And when he cupped her breast with his hand, a little moan sneaked out. All she could do was react.

Maybe she'd known all along that this was coming.

From the moment she'd met Danny, there'd been a powerful attraction. She ruffled his damp hair as his lips trailed from her neck to her collarbone. He drifted lower still, until he could tease at her nipple through the wet fabric of her bra.

Pleasure washed over her, so intense that she felt as if she were drowning in sensation. Jordan closed her eyes and threw out her arms, floating on the surface as he gently explored her body with his hands and his mouth. It felt like total surrender, as if the real world no longer existed. She had no worries, no doubts and nothing holding her back. She was a woman, from the tips of her toes to the top of her head, and for the first time in her life, she was truly comfortable with it.

And then a familiar sound echoed through the cavernous room. Jordan opened her eyes and groaned softly.

"Ignore it," he said, pulling her up into his embrace.

"I can't."

"What could be so imp—"

"It's probably my father. He calls every Friday about this time for a progress report. If I don't answer he gets—well, he doesn't like it." She carefully untangled herself from Danny's embrace and walked over to the edge of the pool. Bracing her hands on the edge, she boosted herself onto the deck, then retrieved her phone.

"Hello, Daddy," she said, hurrying to the stairs and away from the echo of the pool. In truth, she was almost happy for the interruption. Things were moving far too fast with Danny and she needed a chance to take a breath.

From now on, she was going to think before she ripped off her clothes and gave in to the charms of a naked Irishman.

3

DANNY WOKE UP with a start, yanked out of a deep and dreamless sleep. The dogs were at the front door of the caretaker's cottage, barking frantically. He swung his legs over the edge of the bed and stood, wondering what had set them off. Dragging the sheet along with him, he wrapped it around his naked body.

"Shush," he said, walking out of the bedroom and flipping on the lights. "What are you two about?"

A frantic rap sounded on the door and he opened it to find Jordan standing on the other side. She was dressed in just a T-shirt and her panties, her feet bare.

Pushing past him, she stalked inside, then spun around to face him. "Were you just in the house?" she asked.

He looked at her and shook his head, trying to reconcile her strange appearance at his door. "What time is it?"

"I—I don't know. Late. Maybe two?" Her expression was etched with fear. "Were you just in the house?"

Danny raked his hand through his hair. "No. I was asleep."

"Don't lie to me," she snapped.

"What the hell are you talking about, Jordan? After you left, I came right back here. I've been here ever since. Though not by choice."

"Someone was in my bedroom," she said. "I was having trouble sleeping and I turned over and opened my eyes and he was standing in the doorway. I could see him."

Danny reached out and drew her into his arms. "It was probably just a nightmare."

"No!" she cried, shoving away from him. "I reached out to turn on the light and then he was gone. But I heard his footsteps in the hall. I ran out to follow him, but there was no one there."

"Sometimes your mind can play tricks on you."

"I know what I saw."

"The doors were locked. How could anyone have gotten in the house?"

She drew a ragged breath, then sighed softly, sinking against his body. "I—I don't know. I was just so—I was sure I—"

Danny smoothed his hand over her hair and drew her closer. "Do you want me to go back and search the house for you? I'll take the dogs. If there's anyone in the house, Finny and Mogue will find them."

"No. I'm fine."

"You can stay here with me, if you like. We'll look into this tomorrow."

She glanced up at him, eyes wide. "I can't stay here."

"Why not? Nothing is going to happen." He took her hand, lacing his fingers through hers, then drew her along toward the bedroom. "I'll stay on my side of the bed and you have to promise to stay on your side."

"I don't know," she murmured. "Maybe I should take my chances in the house."

"Your choice," Danny said with a shrug. "I can send the dogs back with you. They'll protect you."

"Maybe that would be best," she replied.

Danny couldn't think of anything he wanted more than to have Jordan in his bed. From the moment they'd first kissed it had been all he could think about. But it had to be on her terms. Since her father's call, she'd been a bit more aloof and he knew exactly what she was thinking. Having an affair with him would probably break all kinds of rules that she couldn't afford to break.

"I'll walk you back and make sure everything is all right." He strode into the bedroom, grabbed his jeans and tugged them on. Then he pulled his jacket from the bedpost and when he returned to her, draped it over her shoulders. "Come on, let's go."

As they walked outside into the chilly night, he whistled softly to the dogs and they fell into step behind them.

"You probably think I'm crazy," she said.

"No. Does anyone else have a key to the house? Did you ever give one to any of the workmen?"

"No. I've always been very careful. And I lock the temporary doors from the inside with a padlock. There's no way to get in once I've locked everything."

They walked through the dark house. He could feel her tense beside him and he slipped his arm around her shoulders and pulled her close. When they reached her bedroom, he walked inside first. "I thought you said you turned on the light."

"I did," she said. "At least, I think I did. Maybe this was just all a dream."

Danny turned on the bedside lamp, then carefully surveyed the room. There didn't seem to be anything amiss. "Come on, hop in."

The dogs explored the room as Jordan crawled back into bed and pulled the covers up to her chin. Danny sat down on the edge of the bed. "The dogs will bark if anyone comes into the house."

"Stay here a little longer," Jordan said.

"Sure. Do you have any whiskey? Maybe a drink would calm your nerves."

"There is a bottle downstairs."

"I'll go get it and check all the doors and windows. You stay here with the dogs."

Jordan turned onto her side and clutched his hand. "I feel so stupid. It was probably just a bad dream. I had that curry for dinner and I always have weird dreams after spicy food." She looked up at him. "I'm sorry I bothered you."

"It's not a problem," he said. He dropped a kiss on her lips, not really thinking before he did. She was so close, it just seemed like the most natural thing to kiss her. But as soon as he drew back, Danny realized that one kiss would not be enough. "I'll be back in a few minutes."

The house was silent as Danny walked through the lower floor, checking the windows and the doors. He had to believe that Jordan had seen *something* to send her running to him in the middle of the night. When he checked the library, he noticed one of the windows was open a crack and shut it. But before he turned out the light, he spotted a muddy footprint on the floor near one of the bookshelves.

It was the print of a man's shoe or boot, a bit larger than his own, with a different pattern on the sole. Bending down, Danny ran his finger over the footprint and found the mud still damp. "What the hell," he muttered. Someone *had* been in the house, and not very long ago.

He grabbed the bottle of whiskey from the table in the library, along with two glasses and headed upstairs. For now, he'd keep his discovery a secret. It wouldn't do to scare Jordan. But he had no intention of leaving her alone in the house now—with or without his dogs.

When he returned to the bedroom, Danny found her sitting up in bed, Finny and Mogue curled up beside her. He chuckled softly as he handed her a glass and poured whiskey into it. "I usually don't let them sleep on the bed." He snapped his fingers and the dogs jumped down to the floor. Danny sat down beside her and poured himself a glass.

"Did you find anything?" she asked.

Danny shook his head. "No. Everything was locked up tight. But I'm going to stay here tonight with you anyway. Just to be certain." He wrapped his arm around her shoulders and pulled her up against his body.

She relaxed, resting her whiskey on his stomach as she nestled into the curve of his body. Danny sipped at his drink as he rubbed her shoulder, his palm smoothing over her silken skin. His thoughts focused on that part of her body then drifted back to their swim in the pool.

How much would it take to get them back to that

moment, to that instant when their eyes met and the world seemed to stand still? He nuzzled his face in her hair then pressed a kiss to her forehead. He wasn't going to go there. Not until she was ready.

"Feel better?" he asked.

"Yes," she said.

The whiskey warmed his belly and relaxed his body. But it only made the thoughts of her more intense. He ran his hand over her arm and she turned in to him, her warmth seeping through the jeans he'd pulled on. It wasn't enough just to touch her.

Danny leaned over and pressed his mouth to hers, his tongue slowly tracing the crease between her lips. When he drew back, she was watching him. They stared at each other for a long time, neither one of them moving or speaking. Then Jordan pushed up on her elbow, her hand slipping around his neck to draw him near.

A long, soft kiss was his reward for his patience. And when she finally drew back, he knew that they'd started where they'd left off earlier. In fact, to his surprise, she'd decided to jump ahead a few steps.

She worked the buttons open on his jeans, then ran her hand from his belly to his chest and back again. Her touch sent his senses reeling and he wasn't sure if he could maintain his control at this kind of pace.

When her hand dipped lower, Danny groaned. It had been a while since the last time he'd had a woman. And he'd never had any trouble taking care of a woman's needs before his own. But this woman could do things to him that had never been done before.

He waited, holding his breath, as her hand slipped beneath the waistband of his jeans. Danny was almost afraid to touch her, afraid that just the simple feel of her flesh beneath his fingers would send him over the edge. She still wore the T-shirt and panties and he was almost grateful that she was covered.

But that gratitude didn't last long. Suddenly, she got to her knees and pulled the T-shirt over her head, tossing it aside. Danny's breath caught in his throat. She was, by all standards, the most beautiful creature he'd ever seen.

He quickly stripped off his jeans and she rid herself of her panties. When they were both naked, she sat next to him, as if she wasn't sure how to proceed. "I've never been much good at this," she whispered.

"I find that very hard to believe."

"If I'm doing something wrong, I want you to tell me. Promise?"

He shook his head. "We'll show each other," he said. "Take my hand." She did as she was told. "Show me where you like to be touched." Slowly, she placed his hand on her breast.

That was all it took to start them down a path of undeniable pleasure. That simple contact, the soft weight of her flesh in his hand, the stiff peak of her nipple, sent waves of desire racing through his body.

A sigh slipped from her throat and Danny pulled her down next to him and captured her mouth in a kiss filled with overwhelming need.

He pulled her beneath him, drawing her legs up alongside his hips. She was soft and warm, every inch of her naked body like a revelation. Had he ever felt this kind of need before? Had he ever been so determined to possess a woman?

Though he wanted to lose himself inside her, Danny realized that he'd left the condoms back at the caretaker's cottage. He weighed the risks of leaving her, knowing how easily the connection between them could snap. There were other ways to satisfy them both.

He moved against her, his shaft sliding along the moist slit between her legs. Jordan gasped, arching against him in response, her breath quickening. Danny closed his eyes, enjoying the sensations racing through his body. It was as close to sex as they could get without actually having sex and he thought it would be enough.

But for Jordan, it wasn't. She shifted beneath him and his next thrust was met with a different kind of resistance. He slipped inside her once, then quickly withdrew.

"I have condoms," he murmured. "But they're back in the cottage. I can go get them."

"I have condoms. And they're in the bedside table. I bought them after we met," she admitted.

Danny stretched out on top of her and opened the drawer, then grabbed the box. He quickly sheathed himself and a few seconds later, slipped back between her legs. He kissed her softly, his hands braced on either side of her shoulders, his shaft gently probing at her damp entrance.

It took every ounce of his willpower to wait, to move against her without plunging deep. But with every stroke, she seemed to grow more impatient, her moans tinged with frustration. And when he finally gave in, the sensation of entering her warmth nearly sent him over the edge.

Danny sensed she was close and every now and

then, he pulled out and rubbed up against her for a time, before slipping back inside.

Jordan's breath quickened and he continued to tease her until she was clutching at his shoulders and delirious with need. When the first shudder wracked her body, he knew that he could finally relinquish control.

Jordan arched against him, crying out as her body convulsed in a deep and powerful orgasm. He felt her tighten around him and drove into her one last time, then let himself go, his orgasm exploding deep inside her.

They continued to rock together, slowing the pace as the intensity of their pleasure subsided. It had been so quick, yet so powerful, nothing at all like he'd planned. He'd imagined a long, slow seduction, a gentle teasing before complete surrender.

This had been nothing more than a headlong rush toward mutual orgasms.

Danny pulled her down on top of him then rolled to his side until they faced each other. "Whoever told you that you weren't good at that ought to have the shite beat out of him on a daily basis."

"I think he might have been compensating for his own shortcomings," Jordan said.

"Shortcomings? Really?"

"Yeah," she said. "Really short shortcomings."

As he wrapped her in his arms and tucked her body into the curve of his, Danny found a certain satisfaction in the notion that he'd been the best. It was a good place to begin.

THE END OF DANNY'S FIRST WEEK of work was cause for celebration, at least according to him. In Jordan's mind, they'd been celebrating every night in her bedroom. There hadn't been any question where he'd sleep at night and each evening, after a late dinner and a sunset hike along the cliffs, they'd climb the stairs and begin a lazy night of lovemaking.

Jordan glanced over at him as he steered the car through the narrow streets of Ballykirk. Though she would have been happy to find their fun between the sheets, Danny had insisted that they go out. His brother Riley was singing at the family pub and everyone would be there.

He pulled the Land Rover into the narrow lane behind the blacksmith shop and stopped it. "Now, don't worry about meeting the family. You already know Kell, though I think he's back in Dublin this week. Oh, and Ma and Da are still in Scotland. But you'll like Riley. And his fiancée, Nan, is American, so you'll have that in common."

"I'm not nervous," she said. "Why would I be nervous?"

He shrugged. "You shouldn't be. It's just that the pub can be a wee bit…well, everyone will be happy to meet you, I can promise that." He jumped out of the car and jogged around to her side, then opened her door. "You look beautiful, by the way."

She took his hand and got out of the car. "Thank you."

He let the dogs out of the back, then slipped his arm around her waist. "I know this won't be anything like the clubs you go to in New York but you'll have fun, I promise. We're going to dance and sing and have a few pints. And at the end of the night, I'm going to take you home and make love to you."

"Can't we just skip to the last part? I'm really not much of a party girl."

"If you don't like it, we'll leave. But I promise, I'm going to show you a good time."

"Then let's go," Jordan said. "I'm ready...I think."

The pub was noisy and crowded when they walked inside. Danny wrapped his arm around her shoulders and guided her through the crowd, calling out greetings to friends as he passed. Jordan pasted a smile on her face and tried to appear friendly.

Suddenly, a beautiful dark-haired girl appeared out of the crowd. "You're here!" she cried. "And you've brought a friend."

"Nan Galvin, this is Jordan Kennally. My boss and my—"

"His friend," Jordan interrupted, holding out her hand.

Nan took Jordan's hand and gave it a firm shake. "Hello. I'm Nan. Tiernan, actually, but everyone calls me Nan. I'm the soon-to-be sister-in-law. Not *so* soon. New Year's Eve. You're American. Kellan didn't mention that. He also didn't mention how pretty you are."

"Yes, I'm from New York. And—and thank you."

"Madison, Wisconsin," Nan said. "Come on, I'll get you a drink. Do you like margaritas? No one knew how to make them here. Can you imagine that? I guess they're not very Irish. Now, everyone is drinking them. I'm not a fan of Guinness. It makes me burp."

Nan took Jordan's hand and led her to the bar. She

glanced back and waved at Danny and he grinned. "How long have you been in Ireland?" Jordan asked.

"Since July." She paused and smiled. "I rented the Quinn family cottage for my vacation and decided to stay for the rest of my life. What about you?"

"I've been here for sixteen months."

"Really? That's a long time. Then I'm sure you've been to plenty of pubs."

"Just for the occasional meal," Jordan said. "I didn't really get out much…until Danny."

"Well, then, we'll have to make sure you have a grand time, won't we?" When they reached the bar, Nan shooed a man off his bar stool and offered it to Jordan. When their drinks arrived, she handed the margarita to Jordan and gave a toast.

"To the mighty Quinn brothers. The sexiest men in all of Ireland."

Jordan clinked her glass against Nan's then took a sip. The other woman wasn't at all what she had expected. Her dark hair was cropped short and curled around her face, and though she wore barely any makeup, she was strikingly beautiful in a pure and natural way. "Danny said you're engaged to his brother Riley. I haven't met him. I know Kellan, but not him."

"He's over there, on stage singing." She took a sip of her drink, then set it down. "I would warn you off about the Quinn brothers, but I think it would be wonderful for Danny to find someone."

"Oh!" Jordan was startled. "No, it's not like that. I can't fall in love with him. I'm leaving in a month."

Nan smiled. "Of course you can't. That's what I said, too."

"I'm sure that I won't—"

"Enough of this!" Danny appeared out of the crowd and took Jordan's hand. "I want to dance, woman. And there's no one in this place that I want in my arms but you. Will ya dance with me, Jordan?"

Jordan looked back and forth between Danny and Nan. Though she'd prefer to sit quietly at the bar sipping a drink, this talk of love was too much. She'd known Danny less than a week. "I'm not sure I know how," Jordan said, turning back to Danny.

"It's simple," he said. "I'll teach you."

Nan gave Jordan a wave before she disappeared into the crush of people on the dance floor. They walked past the stage and Jordan stopped to watch the singer. Riley Quinn looked like his two brothers, with the same dark hair and pale-blue eyes, the same devilish smile and to-die-for body.

Danny pulled her into his arms. "Just follow me," he said. And off they went, spinning and stepping around the floor to the crazy rhythm of the music. They bumped into a lot of people, but that seemed to be part of the fun. Gradually, Jordan picked up the steps and before long, she didn't have to think about her feet at all.

They danced three songs before the tempo slowed to a quiet ballad. Danny drew her close and wrapped his arms around her waist. "Are you having a good time?" he murmured, his breath warm against her ear.

Jordan nodded. "I am. I've never really danced like that."

"And now that you have, what would you like to do next?"

"I'd like to kiss you," she said. "But I don't think that would be a good idea."

He brushed his lips against hers. "I think it's a grand idea. What next?"

"I'd like you to do that again, with just a little more... tongue."

He did as she asked, capturing her lips with his and slowly tracing them with his tongue. He lingered for a bit, then kissed her deeply and Jordan sank against him, her knees going weak.

The sound of the music and the crowd faded around them and Jordan lost herself in the rush of desire that overwhelmed her body. It had become so easy to need him, and yet it frightened her at the same time.

She hadn't been prepared to feel this way, to completely surrender to emotion and physical need. But she couldn't help herself. His touch, his taste, it had become an addiction too overwhelming to resist. When he touched her she felt beautiful and powerful, as if everything in the world were hers to enjoy.

"What else?" he murmured, his lips damp on her cheek.

"I want you to run your hands over my body like you did this morning before we got out of bed. I want to feel your lips on my skin. And I want you to take all my clothes off and I want to take all of your clothes off and—"

"Stop," he growled.

"Why?"

"Because if you keep talking like that, I'm going to have to leave the pub with a bar tray over my lap."

Jordan arched against him, her hips meeting his and he groaned again. "Just from talking?"

"You have that effect on me," Danny said.

"Maybe we should take a walk and get some air," Jordan said. "We'll cool off a little bit."

"And that's a fine idea. Lead the way."

He grabbed her waist and gently pushed her along through the crowd, walking behind her. When they reached the front door, Danny held it open and they both stepped outside onto the street. "Come with me," he murmured.

"Where are we going now?"

"Some place where we can be alone." He pulled her into the doorway of a shop and kissed her again, his body blocking her view of the street. His fingers skimmed along her waist, then worked at the buttons of her dress. When he finally cupped her breast in his palm, he moaned softly. "Jaysus, I need you. I've never needed a woman like I need you right now." He grabbed her hand and pulled her out of the doorway. "We can't stay here."

When they passed an alleyway, he pulled her into the shadows and pressed her back against a brick wall, parting the front of her dress until he found her nipple with his mouth. He teased at the peak through the lacy fabric of her bra. Jordan's breath caught in her throat and she sighed, waves of delicious sensation coursing through her body.

His hand slid beneath her skirt and before she could catch her breath, he touched the damp spot between her legs. Jordan arched against him and he gently stroked her through her panties. She was already on the edge and it didn't take much more to make her shudder with pleasure.

Jordan tried to occupy her mind with something else, work, plans, schedules. But it was no use. He was determined to prove his power over her. She tipped her head back, her fingers clutching at his shoulders. And then, her body throbbed and wave after wave of sensation coursed through her. A moan slipped from her lips and though she knew they might be discovered at any moment, Jordan didn't care.

When the last spasm died in her body, Jordan looked up at Danny and found him smiling. He touched his lips to hers in a gentle kiss. "Sorry about that," he murmured. "I didn't realize you were so close."

"Neither did I," Jordan whispered.

"Can you walk?"

She nodded. He took her hand again and led her out of the shadows. Her legs felt boneless and it was all she could do to put one foot in front of the other. They walked past the bakery and then found the path that led to the smithy.

Finny and Mogue were sleeping on the stoop and they raised their heads as Danny opened the front door. The moment the door latched shut behind them, Jordan knew what she wanted. With frantic fingers, she stripped off her clothes and then started on Danny's.

They stumbled to the bedroom and by the time they reached the bed, they were both naked. Jordan pulled him down on top of her. How had she gone her whole adult life and never felt this desperation, this overpowering need?

He moved to find a condom in the bedside table,

but Jordan stopped him. It was her turn this time. She wanted to watch him, to bring him to his climax, to memorize his every reaction without losing herself in her own pleasure.

"Don't," she whispered. "We won't need them. Not yet." Jordan trailed a line of kisses down his chest, stopping at his belly.

Danny's fingers tangled in her hair. "What are you about?"

"You'll see," she murmured, wrapping her fingers around his stiff shaft. "Just relax. I'll take care of everything…"

"DANNY BOY!"

The shouts echoed through the empty interior of the Speckled Hound as Danny stepped inside the pub. His father was serving breakfast to the Unholy Trinity—Markus Finn, Dealy Carmichael and Johnnie O'Malley—three pensioners who were regular customers at the Hound. Kellan and Riley were sitting on the opposite end of the bar, reading the newspaper.

"There's our boy," Riley shouted. "What's brought you back here so soon?"

"Never left," Danny said. "We spent the night at my place rather than drive back."

"Too much of the black stuff?" Kellan asked.

"Something like that," Danny said. He sat down at the bar. "Can I get a couple of cups of coffee to take away and some soda bread? Warmed up. And toss some butter in the bag."

"Where's the girl?"

"Still asleep," he said.

Kellan looked up from the paper. "You've got yourself a girl?"

"Sure and he has," Riley said. "Brought her to the pub last night, though they only stayed for three dances. Then they started snogging on the dance floor and a few minutes later they were gone."

Nan came out of the kitchen, a coffee mug in her hand. Her expression brightened when she saw Danny. "Good morning, you! Is Jordan with you? I forgot to tell her last night that she should come to our engagement party. You'll tell her, won't you?"

"Wait a bloody minute," Kellan said, glancing between Nan and Riley and Danny. "This girl, the one you were snogging. It's Jordan?"

Danny winced. "Well, yes. That would be correct. Jordan and I are…involved."

"You've been working for her for five feckin' days," Kellan shouted. "How the hell is that possible?"

"Don't ask me," Danny said. "I'm as surprised as you. But there's no problem."

"You're sleeping with your boss," Kellan said.

"Not actually. She's not my boss. She's my muse." Eamon Quinn walked out of the kitchen, a coffeepot in his hand. Danny turned to him, anxious for a change of subject. "Hello, Da. How was your holiday?"

"Oh, it was grand. Got back late last night. You know how your ma loves Scotland. We expected to be back a few days ago, but there was another festival that Maggie just had to see. Bought a kilt, she did. What does a good Irish girl need with a bleedin' kilt? It's sacrilege, it is."

"I like the girl," Nan said, sitting down next to Riley.

"What girl?" Eamon asked.

"Danny's new girlfriend," Nan replied. "Or his boss. Or his muse." She giggled. "Take your pick. She's very pretty. But then, all American girls are pretty, don't you think?"

Danny grinned. "Yes, they are. You should visit Castle Cnoc and see the work she's done on the manor house. I'm sure she'd give you a tour."

"That would be lovely," Nan said. "It will give me another chance to convince her of your fine qualities and noble ambitions."

"I do believe our brother is in love," Riley teased. "Look at him. He looks besotted. He's got that well satisfied look. And he can't keep himself from smiling."

Danny shook his head. It *was* hard to keep from grinning when the only thing going through his head was thoughts of Jordan…naked…asleep in his bed. "I'm not in love," Danny assured them all. "I've only known her less than a week. And you're the besotted one in this family, Riley."

"Well, I'm happy he's found a nice girl," Eamon declared. "It's about bloody time. I was starting to wonder if any of you lot would ever settle down." He walked over to the Unholy Trinity and leaned against the bar. "We made the bet on Riley and Nan. What say we put some money on Danny and this new girl?"

"You're gambling on my love life?" Danny asked.

"We've grown bored with wagering on Dealy's ability to catch fish," Markus said. "And it's not nearly as interesting as your ability to catch women."

"Can I get in on this?" Riley asked. "What's the wager? How much are we tossing in?"

Kellan shook his head. "For a total wanker, Riley,

you managed to get yourself a great woman. Don't feck it up or you'll go back to being a total wanker." Kellan turned to Danny. "As for you, watch yourself. I happen to be fond of Jordan and I don't want you hurting her."

"Is that jealousy I hear?" Riley asked.

"No, I just know my little brother. And he doesn't have the best reputation. Jordan is a nice person. She doesn't deserve a git like you." He stood and grabbed his newspaper, then took it and his cup of coffee to a table in the corner.

"You know what your problem is, Danny boy?" Dealy asked. "You're too damn good-looking. Riley and Kellan too. Look at Markus here. Look at that face. When he was a lad, the girls didn't have such high expectations when it came to him. They knew he'd have to work harder because he was so close to ugly."

"Who are you to talk?" Markus said. "You're ugly as a bucket of toads."

"It's true," Johnnie said. "When a lad is too *flash,* he thinks he can get any girl. He's never satisfied with the one he has."

"I'm perfectly satisfied," Riley said.

"So am I," Danny added.

"Don't you get too comfortable," Kellan shouted from across the room. "It won't take her long to see her mistake. You just can't go draggin' anyone off to bed and expect them to fall in love with you."

"I didn't drag her into bed," Danny said. "In fact, she came to me. How could I refuse?" That wasn't exactly the full story. But what had he been supposed to do? She'd been frightened and uneasy and he'd just calmed her nerves in the best way that he could.

Kellan set his paper down and crossed the bar, leaning close to Danny, his voice low. "She looks like she's tough and like she's got herself together," he said, "but she's a lot more fragile than that."

"I know," Danny said. "And I'm not going to hurt her. That's the last thing in the world I'd ever want to do."

"You don't understand. She doesn't work like other people. She has this way of pulling you in, until all you want to do is make her happy. I've seen her do it. And if you fail, she doesn't yell or curse. She just acts all disappointed and then you feel lower than an earthworm's arse."

Danny nodded. "I know, I know." In truth, he didn't know. He hadn't experienced that moment with Jordan. And he didn't mean to anytime soon.

Eamon Quinn walked through the doors from the kitchen with a paper bag. "Here's your breakfast. Two black coffees and soda bread. I threw some fruit salad in there. And before you leave town, you may want to stop by and wish your mother a happy birthday. Tell her she doesn't look a day over thirty-five," he said.

Danny winced. "I'm sorry. I forgot all about her birthday today. I'll ring her later. I've been so—"

"Don't worry. Kellan told her all about your new job. You know, she's been dying to get a look inside that castle, too. You might invite her for a tour to make up for the missed birthday."

"I will," Danny said. "Once it's all finished, I'm sure Jordan wouldn't mind."

"Remember what I said," Kellan muttered.

Danny nodded. "I have to go." He grabbed the bag

and headed out the front door of the pub. As he strode back to his cottage, he drew a deep breath of the sea air and smiled to himself. Funny how his life had changed so much in just five days.

It didn't matter to him how long it lasted. He was going to enjoy himself while he could. And when it was time for Jordan to leave, he'd kiss her goodbye and regret that it couldn't go on for just a little longer.

But even as he told himself it was just a passing thing, Danny could imagine them together for more than just a few weeks or months. He found her endlessly fascinating. And she seemed to find him interesting as well. There was a lot to be said for that, wasn't there?

Danny hurried back to his cottage. The dogs were waiting and he shooed them out, then closed the door. A moment later, Jordan rushed out of the bedroom, half-dressed, her hair tumbling around her face.

"Where have you been?"

"I just went to get us breakfast," he said.

"We're late. I have to get back to the house. The workmen will be there and I have calls to make and—"

"It's Saturday," Danny said.

"I know it is. I work on Saturday. So do you. Just because we're sleeping together doesn't mean we can ignore our responsibilities."

She'd gone from lover back to boss—and she was disappointed in him. "I wasn't gone that long. I was talking to my brothers. Kellan was at the pub and my da was back from his holiday."

"You should have told me you were leaving," she said. "I woke up and you weren't there. I looked all over for you and—"

"You knew I wasn't far," Danny said, frowning. "Jordan, I wouldn't have left you here. I knew we had to get back. So come on, then. Get dressed. Let's go. You're the boss."

Jordan blinked, her expression suddenly shifting. "Don't say that."

"What? That you're the boss?"

She cursed softly. "I'm sorry. I'm really tired and I'm a little hungover and I just want a shower and a really big cup of coffee."

He took one of the paper cups out of the bag. "I brought you coffee," he said. Stepping closer, Danny dropped a kiss on her lips. "And something to eat."

Jordan groaned. "See. I'm really awful. You're right. I need to learn to relax. Why can't I do that? It's Saturday. We should just go right back to bed."

"I shouldn't have left you alone in a strange house."

"Well, don't do it again. Or I'll have to make a note in your personnel file."

Reaching out, he ran a finger along her arm, tracing a lazy path from her wrist to her elbow and back again. "You have a file on me? What does it say?"

She took a sip of her coffee and then sighed. "It says that you have trouble separating work from—from everything else, and I think that might become a problem."

He stared at her for a long moment, fighting back a surge of frustration. Would it always come back to this? Did they always have to be boss and employee? Why couldn't she see them as just a man and a woman? "Am I supposed to pretend that I don't want you? Because I do. All the time. And if that's a problem, then write it up in my personnel file. In big red letters." He walked to the door and pulled it open. "I'll be in the car with Finny and Mogue. As soon as you're ready, we'll go."

Danny snapped his fingers as he walked out the front door, and the dogs came running. He opened the rear door of the Land Rover and they hopped inside. Then, he slid in behind the wheel and waited, his anger growing with every moment that passed.

When she finally came out of the cottage, Jordan walked slowly toward the vehicle. She got into the passenger seat and looked over at him. "I'm sorry," she said. "This is all kind of new to me and I haven't figured out how to handle it yet. You might be able to separate work and pleasure, but I'm going to have to work on it a little longer."

"Then forget about the job. Don't worry. I will get it done and it will be perfect. You have to trust me. We *can* just be lovers."

She nodded, then reached out and grabbed his shirt, pulling him closer. Jordan pressed her face into his chest. "I really hope so."

4

DANNY STARED AT THE ornate medallion he'd begun for the garden gate. He'd been working on it for three days, fitting it in between the hinges and hardware on Jordan's list. He'd carefully copied the design from an old black-and-white photo that Jordan had given him.

The work was beautiful, but it wasn't Irish. He suspected the original artisan was John Wellston, a British blacksmith from Galway who had done a lot of the work in the area at the turn of the century. Wellston's work was quite prized nowadays, found on many historical homes.

At the time Wellston worked, Ireland was in the midst of a rebellion, an attempt to break away from British rule. Wellston worked for many of the wealthy British families and Irish loyalists. But now that Ireland was free, it didn't seem right to put his work back up on the gate. It should be Irish work on an Irish gate.

Danny glanced at his watch, then dropped the tongs on the floor and shrugged his stiff shoulders. Jordan was out for the morning, running errands to Cork and Bantry. She'd been buying furniture for the house—

keeping a careful inventory of it in a huge book in the library.

She'd been trying to track down some of the original furnishings so she might buy them back. But she hadn't had much luck in that area. Everything she bought was carefully restored and reupholstered, then shipped to a storage facility in Cork, awaiting the moment when it would be moved to Castle Cnoc.

Danny grabbed a towel from the worktable and rubbed the sweat off his grimy face, then grabbed the medallion and hauled it outside, propping it up against an old wooden crate. Drawing a deep breath, he stretched his arms over his head, working the kinks out of his back as he stared at his work.

No, it didn't look better in the light of day. He sat down on a wooden stool set against the wall of the laundry. There wasn't much good about it, he mused. Copying Wellston's work just didn't seem right. He ought to just start over, with a design of his own. At least he'd take some pride in the making of it.

Sighing softly, Danny raked his hands through his hair, then leaned back against the wall, drawing a deep breath of the late-morning breeze.

This had become a sticky point between him and Jordan and it was about to come to a head. They'd disagreed on a few other small projects and he'd given in, agreeing to make exact copies rather than put his own mark on the work.

But the medallion would be the focal point of the walled garden. It needed to match the beauty of the house and the surrounding landscape—and it should be Irish. Maybe he could use that point to convince Jordan.

But first, he'd have to come up with a better design, one with some of the elements of the first, only in a more Gaelic manner.

A wave of exhaustion came over him and Danny fought back a yawn. It didn't help his creativity when he could barely put a thought together. Late nights with Jordan followed by early mornings at the forge were wearing on him. And though he kept assuring Jordan he was right on schedule, that wasn't the truth. He'd fallen at least a week behind and was falling further with every day that passed.

He closed his eyes and let his mind drift, searching for inspiration. But instead, his mind filled with thoughts of Jordan, her naked body, her lush mouth, her warm hands—disconnected images of pleasure that plagued him night and day.

Danny cursed beneath his breath. She had become his *leanan sidhe,* so alluring and yet so dangerous, tempting him and tormenting him at the very same time. He was a happier man when she was close, but was it worth the price he paid? He felt as if she'd already stolen a part of his soul, and the thought of taking it back brought out only a desperate ache deep inside of him.

Wanting her had become second nature, like drawing breath. He couldn't look at her without his hands aching to touch her, or his lips craving her taste. Was this simple lust or obsession? He was so wrapped up in it, Danny couldn't tell the difference, not that he'd even know in the first place. If he could just get a decent night's sleep, then maybe he could sort it all out.

But the nights were what he was living for. With

every one spent with Jordan, he learned more and more
about passion and need, grew more aware of the pleasure they could give each other. Her bed had become
a place to explore and experiment, a place to push the
boundaries of what was possible between a man and a
woman.

Danny drew a deep breath and let his body relax. Just
a few minutes, a short kip, and he'd find his energy. He
couldn't be bothered to walk back to his cottage or even
stretch out on the grass at his feet. Just a few…

"Are you asleep?"

Startled by her voice, Danny sat up straight and
opened his eyes. "No," he said, wiping his eyes. "No, I
was just thinking."

"You were asleep," Jordan said, her brow furrowed
deeply.

"Yes," he admitted. "Maybe I was. I'm knackered,
Jordan. Give me a break. I just needed a quick kip and
then back to work."

"How are you supposed to stay on schedule if you're
napping on the job?" There was an edge to her voice
and he could see she was upset.

He grinned and held out his hand to her. "How am I
supposed to stay on schedule if I'm spending my nights
pleasing you? That would be the more appropriate question."

"Are you saying I don't work?" Jordan asked.

He shook his head. How did she get that out of his
comment? "Of course not. I'm saying that what we do
in our spare time makes it hard to get anything done
during the day. You can sleep in but I have to get up
and go to work."

"You *are* saying I don't work!" Jordan began to pace back and forth in front of him. With every step she took, she was getting more and more upset and Danny stood silently, searching for a way to defuse the looming argument.

"Would you like to tell me what you're really upset about?"

She stopped and opened her mouth, then snapped it shut. "No," she said.

He reached out and grabbed her hand. "Come on, sit down and tell me about your day."

She plopped down on the stool and cupped her chin in her hand. "I bought a crystal vase a few months ago. It's an exact match for one that was pictured in the foyer. I put it in the butler's pantry and now it's gone. It just disappeared. I have no idea how long it's been gone, but I didn't imagine that I bought it or put it there. I have a receipt." She rubbed her forehead. "Sometimes I think I'm going crazy."

"You're not going crazy," he said.

She shrugged. "I know. One of the workmen must have come into the house and taken it. I need to be more careful with the locks."

"What else?" he asked.

"It's nothing. I'm just tired. Stressed. Confused." She pointed to the medallion. "It looks nice."

"No, it doesn't," Danny said. "I don't like it. The smith who designed it was a Brit. And I refuse to copy his work. There should be Irish work on the gate."

"We had an agreement," Jordan said.

"And I'm going back on it. You want a medallion for the garden gate, I'll make you one. It's going to be beautiful and it will be Irish and it will be my design. I want to leave something of my work in this place."

"I could fire you for this," she said, a defiant tilt to her chin.

He chuckled. "You could. But you won't. You wanted the best and I'm the best."

She shook her head. "Do what you want," she murmured, her voice wavering. "I'm tired, too. And everything is all screwed up. And it's all because of you."

"Me? How am I to blame?"

She looked at him, her eyes filling with tears. She'd gone from contrary to crying in the course of a few seconds. What the hell was he supposed to do now? Danny tried to grab her hand, but she turned and started back to the house.

"Oh, bollocks," he muttered. He ran after her, catching up on the stone terrace. "Jordan, wait." He caught her waist and spun her around to face him. "What's wrong?"

"Nothing," she said, shaking her head. "Just go back to work."

"No. You're in tears."

"I am not!" she cried, denying the wet streaks on her face. "I'm not crying. I don't cry."

"Then why is your face wet?"

"I don't cry!"

"You're tired. We barely got any sleep last night. I was acting like an arse. If you *are* crying, which I'm not saying you are, it wouldn't be a surprise."

"I'm not crying," she insisted.

He pulled her along to a bench and sat down next to her, wrapping his arm around her shoulders and smoothing the hair from her eyes. "Tell me what's going on."

She drew a ragged breath and brushed the tears from her cheeks. "I—I need to be done with this job. I need to go home. I have better things waiting for me and the longer I stay here, the less chance I have of getting them."

Just the mention of her leaving caused a pain, like a dagger to his heart. "So you'll finish the job and go home," he murmured, pulling her close and kissing her temple.

"But the longer I stay here with you, the more I don't want to leave. Everything is so simple here. I don't have to fight to be happy." She sniffled. "Do you know what I was just doing?"

"Threatening to fire me?" Danny teased.

"Talking to my father. He has a project that I really want to manage, a boutique hotel in SoHo. I thought, maybe, when he gave me this job, he was preparing me for that one. It's the perfect project for me and he knows it—small, unique. And I was right on track to get it. Until you."

"You're going to blame this on me?"

"Yes. Because I really don't care that he's probably going to give it to my brother. My brother who wouldn't know a sconce from a scone. I'm just so tired of this constant battle. Here, I'm happy. I don't feel any pressure and I actually like this job. And I like you."

"I like you, too," Danny said. "And I can tell how much this hotel project means to you."

"It doesn't mean anything," Jordan said with a shaky laugh.

"Of course it does. You're just angry." He cupped her face in his hands and touched his lips to hers. "We'll figure this out. You'll find a way to change your father's mind."

"What about the gate?" she asked.

"You have to trust me. You have to let me do this my way. I promise, I'll make it good."

She closed her eyes and sighed, her shoulders sagging. "Just get it done. I don't care how you do it. It doesn't make a difference anymore." Jordan pulled out of his grasp. "I really don't think it's a good idea for us to spend so much time together. Both of us know there isn't a future here. And we should both focus more on work."

"Sure," Danny said.

"Maybe you should stay at the cottage tonight."

"No problem." Danny wanted to grab her and pull her into his arms, to kiss away all her worries. He much preferred complete infatuation to utter confusion. But right now, Jordan needed a bit of space, a chance to figure out what she really wanted. She thought her problem was him; but Danny suspected there was something else at work here, something much deeper.

If she needed time, he'd give her that. She could have all the time she wanted. "Come on," he said. "Let's go make you a cup of tea. That always makes things better."

"I don't like tea," she said.

"What about ice cream?" he asked.

"I love ice cream."

"There's a place in town that has the best strawberry ice cream," he said.

She smiled. "I love chocolate."

"They have that, too," Danny said. "We'll go have ourselves a scoop."

"We should really get back to work."

"Well, if we're going to be spending our nights alone, then we'll have plenty of time for work."

She drew in a ragged breath and forced a smile. "I may have been a bit rash about that. Maybe if we just tried to get to sleep earlier, things would improve."

Danny drew her into his arms and gave her a fierce hug. "We'll give that a try," he said. "Now stop crying and we'll go get ice cream."

"I'm not crying," she insisted, her face pressed into his chest.

"Sure you're not," Danny whispered.

JORDAN STRODE DOWN the garden path, her scheduling flowchart clutched in her hands. It was about time to get this project back on track. No more distractions, no more Ms. Nice Girl.

Maybe she did need to be tougher. Obviously, whoever was stealing from the house thought she was an easy mark. And if that's what it took to get what she wanted, then she'd just have to change her ways. Bartie was a perfect example. He'd been working on the garden for months and nothing was done. Danny was doing his own thing with the gate medallions. And the filter for the pool had been nothing but trouble since it was installed.

"It's time to kick ass and take names," she muttered to herself. "Get tough. Be mean."

Cursing softly, she brushed aside the memory of her

attempt with Danny. The humiliation of breaking down in front of him yesterday still brought a flush of warmth to her cheeks. She'd never let her emotions get the better of her in her business life before. Why now?

She'd just been so overwhelmed with everything that had happened between them that she'd cracked. Too many late nights, too much time spent feeling like a wanton woman rather than a detached professional.

But this wasn't just about the job. Though she'd tried to blame everything on Danny, Jordan knew it was nearly all her fault. Ireland was changing her. She'd lived here for months, feeling like a fish out of water. But now, with Danny's arrival, this place was beginning to feel like home.

If she hadn't been so weak, so anxious to jump into an affair with him, then everything would be fine. He'd be finishing his work and she'd be getting ready to leave Ireland for a better project in Manhattan. And she'd have no regrets for anything that had happened between them.

But Danny had seduced her and at the same time, awakened a part of her that she hadn't known existed. For the first time in her life, she felt needed...wanted... desired. And that made her feel wonderful.

How many times had she heard professional women discussing the problem with trying to have it all? Was this what they meant? Did romance exist in direct competition with professional success? Could she be a woman in love and a woman in business at the same time? Or would one side always suffer?

Of course she could, Jordan mused. Women did it every day. But they didn't have four brothers to compete with, or a father who never seemed to be satisfied. Or a man who could inflame her body with just a simple touch of his hand.

Her job would have been so much easier if Danny Quinn had turned out to be fifty years old, balding and toothless. Instead, he had to be handsome and charming and sexy as sin. She'd never stood a chance. Her feeble attempt to put an end to their late nights had lasted all of about two minutes. Last night had been just as long and adventurous as the previous nights had been.

Jordan turned in to the entrance of the garden and observed the landscape in front of her. More holes. More piles of dirt. It looked as if Bartie and Daisy had turned over every single inch of soil in the garden.

Gathering her resolve, Jordan strode inside the walls and approached the elderly couple. They were bent low, peering into a deep hole. "What are you two looking for?"

They jumped at the sound of her voice and then quickly straightened, fumbling with the tools they held. "Nothing."

"Nothing?" She stepped over and looked into the hole. "If there's nothing, then why are you digging holes?"

"The soil," Bartie said. "Ferrous—"

"Yes, I know. Ferrous metals. I searched *ferrous metals in Irish gardens* on the internet last night. I didn't find anything. Not one thing about iron in the soil. And as far as roses, they can grow in almost any kind of soil with the proper feeding and fertilization."

"Yes," Bartie said, still nodding his head.

"Yes? Is that all you have to say?" Jordan paused

and schooled her temper. "I don't understand what the holdup is. It doesn't look any closer to being done than it did when I arrived here sixteen months ago. Except instead of weeds, I now have piles and piles of dirt."

"Oh, but it is," Bartie said. "I can see how you think that, Miss Kennally. But rose gardens in Ireland can be a tricky thing. The soil has to be prepared in just the right way or you'll have a catastrophe on your hands. We've had to go down a bit deeper than we planned, but it's important. To avoid catastrophe."

"I don't want a catastrophe. I just want flowers. Roses. Get it done. If—if I don't see flowers in this garden by next week, I'll need to hire a professional."

"Yes, miss."

She stalked back to the entrance of the garden, then turned back to Bartie and Daisy. "Have you been inside the house lately, Bartie?"

The old man shifted nervously. "No, miss. I spend all my time in the garden. Why would I have cause to come in the house?"

"What about you, Daisy?"

"No, ma'am."

Jordan shook her head. "Danny says we might have brownies or fairies in the house. Things keep disappearing and then reappearing somewhere else. Do you know anything about that?"

Bartie nodded. "Oh, yes, miss. Sounds like brownies to me," he said. "I'll keep a watch out for them. In the meantime, you might want to leave a little something out for them, miss. A biscuit or two, maybe a slice of tea cake."

"Or you can build a new house for them," Daisy said.

"Build a new house? For an imaginary creature?" Jordan shook her head. "I have to see some positive changes out here soon. It needs to start looking like a garden, not a construction site."

Bartie tipped his hat, then returned to the hole he was digging. Daisy gave him a worried look and Bartie forced a smile. "Flowers," he said.

As Jordan walked through the opening in the wall, she noticed new hinges hanging from the stone columns. Danny was working on the gate but she'd been reluctant to check up on his progress.

She'd accepted his refusal to copy the original gate, but she was afraid she might not like what he'd come up with to replace it. And if she didn't like it, she'd be forced to make him begin again. She started toward the forge, then decided to wait. Trust. She had to trust that he knew what he was doing.

When she got back inside the house, she headed to the library, ready to get to work on her scheduling. There was still the roof on the laundry cottage and the new gravel paving on the drive. She had to check her inventory of furniture and make a final list of the pieces she needed, and she'd have to make some changes due to Danny's slower pace. But there was still a chance to make her final deadline if she could just control her desires.

Jordan sat down at her desk, feeling much better about her options. Grabbing her calendar, she flipped through the next few weeks, searching for a few open days. A trip back to New York would be an excellent way to lobby for the hotel job. She could fly in one day and out the next. Danny could watch over the workmen for her while she was gone.

"Yes," she murmured. There was still time to get everything she wanted. She'd bring her father a full report on the Castle Cnoc renovation, filled with photos and graphs and flowcharts. Her father loved graphs. He would have to see she was the right one. And if he didn't—if he didn't, she'd—

"I'll quit!" she cried, slamming her pen down on the desk.

"Don't say that."

Jordan glanced up to see Kellan Quinn standing in the doorway of the library. "Hello." For a moment, she'd thought it was Danny, all cleaned up and looking like a proper businessman. The brothers looked so much alike. But in reality, Kellan wasn't anything like Danny. He was cool and aloof and completely in control of his emotions. She could depend on Kellan. Danny? Well, she still hadn't figured that out yet.

He stepped through the door. "Hi. How is it going?"

From the moment she'd met Kellan sixteen months ago, she'd liked him. He was talented and thoughtful and possessed as much enthusiasm for the castle as she did. As the project architect, he'd prepared all the plans and drawings for the renovation, making sure everything they kept was sound and anything new was an accurate restoration. Now that it was almost finished, she realized how much she'd miss working with him.

"Things are going really well," she said. "I didn't know you were coming. Are you looking for Danny?"

"No," Kellan said. "I'm looking for you." He handed her an envelope. "My final bill. I know I could have mailed it, but I come with a personal request. Actually, several. Nan wanted me to remind you of the engagement party. She'd like you to come. It's next Friday night at the pub. And she and my mother would like to come and tour Castle Cnoc once it's all finished, if that's all right with you?"

"I'd love to give them a tour." Jordan stood and took the envelope from him. "Sit," she said, pointing to a nearby chair. "Have you had a chance to walk through the house?"

"No, but I want to. It's been a while. When are you bringing in the furniture?"

"Soon," Jordan said. "I've got a few more things that I need to buy. Library books are next on the list." She glanced around. "I have to fill all these shelves. But I want real books, leather-bound with gold leaf."

"Where are you going to go for those?"

"I don't know. London would probably be best. It would be nice if I could put together a real Irish library, though."

"Really? I thought you were going for more of an English manor house."

"I've been convinced that I should approach this from the Irish side. After all, the owner is half-Irish, so there is good reason to go that way. And Danny—"

"Oh, so that's it," Kellan said with a grin. "Danny is pushing the whole Gaelic-pride thing?"

"No. But he's right. This is an Irish house and the decor should reflect that."

"There's a great rare books dealer in Galway," Kellan said. "I'll email you his name. He'll help you find what you need."

"Thanks," she said.

"So, Joe, tell me that Danny has been treating you well. Is it all fair play, then, or has he been a dosser?"

"Fair play," Jordan said, "I think. He's very good at what he does."

Kellan nodded slyly. "I'm sure he is. That's why women love him."

Jordan felt her cheeks warm. "Professionally. He's an excellent blacksmith. We've had a few creative disagreements, but other than that, it's been going quite well."

"I would warn you off," Kellan said, "but I suspect you know what you're doing."

This caused Jordan to laugh out loud. "I have no idea what I'm doing. I'm figuring it out as I go along."

"I will say this—if he hurts you, I'll reef the shite out of him."

"That won't be necessary. If he hurts me, I'll reef the shite out of him myself."

"And if things go well for you both and you'd consider staying in Ireland, then I have a proposal for you."

"A proposal?" Jordan asked.

"I'd like you to consider working with me. I do a lot of houses like this, here and in Europe, and I like your work. And your style. No drama. I don't know the technicalities of getting a work visa, but I'm sure that could be sorted out."

"You're offering me a job?"

"More like a partnership. If you decide to stay."

Jordan leaned back in her chair. She hadn't even considered staying. Her life was back in Manhattan. She had just always assumed she'd return. But it was nice to know that she had options. It would serve her father right if she decided to leave the company. At least *some-one* admired her talent and work ethic. "Thanks," she said. "I'll keep that in mind."

"Everything else is going well?" Kellan asked.

"If you're asking about the house, yes. Oh, except for the brownies or the fairies. We're not sure which we have. And then there's the problems in the garden with Bartie. He's been digging holes for weeks now. Big, deep holes. I don't know what that's all about."

"You have brownies?" Kellan asked.

"Yes," she said. "Someone or something has been sneaking around the house, stealing things and locking doors and windows behind them."

"You do know that brownies aren't real, don't you?"

"Of course she does." Danny appeared at the door, dressed in his leather apron and a backward baseball cap.

"Someone *was* in the house that night," Jordan said. "I know I wasn't dreaming."

Danny drew a deep breath. "Yes, someone was in the house. Maybe not that night, but sometime that day. I found a footprint."

"You did? You didn't tell me that," Jordan said.

"I didn't want to scare you. And you haven't had any more problems since I've been sleeping in the manor house."

"Except for the vase," she said.

"Right, the vase." He smiled. "Well, I think we can rule out the place being haunted. Ghosts don't carry off crystal vases."

Kellan nodded. "Yeah, it was easier to believe in

ghosts when the place looked like a wreck. Some of these old houses have secret entrances. And this house was used during the rebellion to smuggle guns. Maybe that's how your brownies are getting in and out."

Danny grinned. "Really? Where would this secret passage be?"

"I don't know. I have the original blueprints, but there wasn't anything on those. But then, there wouldn't be if it was a secret. I just never thought to look." He stood. "You need to find an undefined space. You could figure it out if you measured the rooms. Somewhere there's a missing meter or so, a space wide enough for a hall or a stairway."

"Now you have me curious," Jordan said, smiling. "Wouldn't that be a tale to tell the owner when she arrives? I think we should start looking. I want to find it."

"I'd love to help," Kellan said, standing, "but I'm off to Dublin. I need to scare up some more work." He crossed the room and held out his hand to Jordan. "It was a pure pleasure working with you, Joe."

Jordan smiled. "And thank you for the offer, Kellan," she said. "I'll think about it."

"Good." Kellan gave Danny a slap on the shoulder as he walked out the door. "You, watch yourself. Don't be an arse. Be nice to your boss."

When they were alone, Danny sat down in the chair Kellan had vacated. "What was that all about?" he asked.

"He brought me his bill," Jordan said.

"That's not what I'm talking about," Danny said. "What kind of offer did Kellan make you?"

"It's nothing," Jordan said. "Just business." She didn't

want Danny to know that she would even consider staying in Ireland. If he hadn't thought about it, then knowing that she had would likely send him running in the opposite direction. And though Kellan's offer was generous, it would take a lot to get her to give up her life in America.

Jordan jumped out of her chair. "I think we should look for that secret passage. Then we can figure out if anyone has been sneaking into the house." She walked over to the wall of shelves. "How are we going to find it?"

"Tap on the walls," Danny suggested. "Look for hidden latches or hinges." He stood and walked to the door. "I have to get back to work. I'll see you later."

Jordan watched him retreat, then frowned. He seemed a bit upset. Maybe she should have told him about Kellan's offer. But there was another reason she'd held back. What if he wanted her to stay?

Jordan drew a deep breath and closed her eyes. She could deny it all she wanted, but she felt something deep and strong for Danny Quinn. It might not be love, but it was something that wouldn't go away just because she wanted it to. Leaving him was going to be much more difficult that she'd ever anticipated.

JORDAN DREW A DEEP BREATH and smiled, a look of pure pleasure coming over her face. "I love the smell of books," she said.

Danny wrinkled his nose and looked around the used bookshop. To him, the store smelled a bit musty. "You and Nan should have come on this trip and left me home."

"Nan?"

Danny nodded. "She was a librarian back in the States. Something to do with old books and maps. She'd have loved this place."

"I thought you wanted to come," Jordan said.

Danny slipped his arms around her waist. "I did. But you were the attraction, not some old moldy books."

"What about when I get old and moldy?" Jordan asked. "Does that mean you're going to stop liking me then?"

Danny nodded. "I'm afraid so. Once you turn thirty, I'm hitting the road."

Jordan gasped, then slapped him playfully. "You're awful. I think I might hate you."

He bent to kiss her neck. "No, you don't. You're mad for me. Admit it. You can't get enough."

She sighed, tipping her head to allow his kisses to continue across her shoulder. "Well, that's true enough. Although, I'm not sure it's a good thing." She gently pushed at his chest. "We're here to look for books," she reminded him. "Not to snog in the stacks."

Reluctantly, Danny let her go. Hand in hand, they strolled down the narrow aisles between the stacks. "What exactly are you looking for?" He reached out and plucked a book from one of the shelves. "Here we go. *An Illustrated History of Faeries and Sprites.* Maybe we can find some of your wee friends in here."

"Why do you think I'm a fairy?" she asked. "I don't have wings. Or a wand."

"Not all fairies look like Tinkerbell. And you wouldn't. You're the kind of fairy that uses all her trickery to lure me in." He pointed to an illustration. "There you are. *Leanan sidhe.* See? That looks just like you."

She examined the illustration carefully. "She has wavy dark hair. That's about it."

"There's more," he said.

"She's naked and I'm fully clothed. And she has wings. And really big boobs."

Danny playfully tugged at the back of her shirt. "You have lovely breasts. And I think I've seen wings in here somewhere. Why don't we just take a closer look?"

"You need to keep your mind on business," she warned, wagging her finger at him.

"And you need to stop distracting me. Fairy magic is a powerful thing and you don't know how powerful you are."

"If I'm so powerful," Jordan said, "why can't I get rid of the brownies in the house?"

"It doesn't work that way. Fairies and brownies exist in separate worlds." He handed her the book. "Here. You can read all about it. I'll buy it for you, *sidhe.*"

"We're here to look for big sets of books with nice leather bindings. And, of course, they should be interesting. I have a lot of shelves to fill."

"So aesthetics are more important than content?"

Jordan shrugged. "I don't know. It all depends. We should get a full set of Shakespeare. Why don't we look for that first?"

"Buying books for their looks is like buying art because it matches the paint on the wall." Danny reached out and plucked a book off the shelf and held it up to her. "You should start with an Irish poet."

"Who is that?"

"W. B. Yeats." Danny leaned back against the bookshelf and closed his eyes. "'When you are old and gray and full of sleep, and nodding by the fire, take down this book, and slowly read, and dream of the soft look your eyes had once, and of their shadows deep.'" He opened his eyes to find her staring at him.

"That's beautiful," she murmured.

"I would still love you when you were old and gray," he murmured. It was an impulsive statement that startled him, as it was based on the assumption that he loved her now—or would in the future. Was that even a possibility in his subconscious? And if it was, what would that mean to her?

Her gaze softened, as if she were searching for the truth in his words. Danny held his breath, hoping that she might return the favor and provide a clue to the depth of her own feelings. Was she falling in love with him? Did she think about a future together?

"You have to have Yeats," Danny finally said, handing her the book.

She drew in a sharp breath and nodded. "Yes. Good."

Danny forced a smile. He'd given her an opening and she hadn't stepped through it. "And you'll need collections of Swift and Goldsmith. And Wilde and Joyce."

"How do you know so much about this?" Jordan asked.

"I'm Irish. We take great pride in our literary heroes. Bram Stoker and Samuel Beckett were Irish, too. And C. S. Lewis. Sister Mary Frances, my high-school English teacher, was a tyrant when it came to homegrown talent. I can still recite 'The Lake Isle of Innisfree.' It was my favorite poem."

If offer card is missing write to: The Reader Service, P.O. Box 1867, Buffalo, NY 14240-1867 or visit us at www.ReaderService.com.

NO POSTAGE
NECESSARY
IF MAILED
IN THE
UNITED STATES

BUSINESS REPLY MAIL

FIRST-CLASS MAIL   PERMIT NO. 717   BUFFALO, NY

POSTAGE WILL BE PAID BY ADDRESSEE

THE READER SERVICE

PO BOX 1867

BUFFALO NY 14240-9952

Play the Lucky Hearts Game

and get...
2 FREE BOOKS and
2 FREE MYSTERY GIFTS...
YOURS TO KEEP!

yes! I have scratched off the gold card.
Please send me my **2 FREE BOOKS** and
2 FREE MYSTERY GIFTS (gifts are worth about $10).
I understand that I am under no obligation to purchase
any books as explained on the back of this card.

Scratch Here!
Then look below to see what your
cards get you...*2 Free Books
& 2 Free Mystery Gifts!*

151/351 HDL FJC2

FIRST NAME

LAST NAME

ADDRESS

APT.#

CITY

STATE/PROV.

ZIP/POSTAL CODE

Visit us online at
www.ReaderService.com

Twenty-one gets you
2 FREE BOOKS and
2 FREE MYSTERY GIFTS!

Twenty gets you
2 FREE BOOKS!

Nineteen gets you
1 FREE BOOK!

TRY AGAIN!

© 2011 HARLEQUIN ENTERPRISES LIMITED. Printed in the U.S.A.
▼ **DETACH AND MAIL CARD TODAY!** ▼

H-B-11/11

"Say it for me," Jordan said.

Danny cleared his throat and stood up straight.

I will arise and go now, and go to Innisfree,
And a small cabin build there, of clay and wattles made;
Nine bean rows will I have there, a hive for the honey-bee,
And live alone in the bee-loud glade.

"That's beautiful," she murmured.

Chuckling, Danny dropped a kiss on her lips. "That's not the end of it. Maybe I'll finish it tonight, when we're in bed."

"Thank you, Sister Mary Frances."

"I used to think that's what I wanted. To escape my family, my brothers mostly, and find a place to be alone, in a bee-loud glade. But I'm starting to realize that life alone wouldn't be much fun."

"Not even in a cabin of clay and waddle? What is waddle?"

"Wattle," Danny said, emphasizing the *t*s. "Wattle is strips of wood held together with clay or mud. Although sometimes, in olden days, they used animal dung and straw."

"You know a lot of trivial things," she said. "I'm impressed."

"What do you know?" Danny asked. "Recite a poem for me."

"No." Jordan laughed. "Outside of nursery rhymes, I'm not sure I know a single poem by memory. Not that

I didn't at one time. Things just seem to come and go from my mind if I don't really think about them."

He leaned into her. "So you'll forget all about me soon enough?"

She slowly shook her head. "No, I don't think I'll ever forget you."

Danny cupped her face in his hands and captured her mouth with his. He loved to kiss Jordan. She was always so sweet and willing, her fingers clutching at his shirt. When he lingered over her lips, she moaned softly and Danny slipped his hand beneath her shirt to caress her breast.

His thoughts returned to the lines of Yeats he'd recited, the words drifting through his head. For the first time in his life, he could imagine spending the rest of his days with one woman. Jordan fascinated him with all her foibles and quirks. At once she was steely, yet vulnerable, serious, yet silly. With every contrast he discovered, he became more and more intrigued. Was this really the woman who could keep him interested for a lifetime?

And then there was their physical compatibility. He'd always enjoyed sex, but sex with Jordan was so much more than the simple satisfying of a need. It was how they communicated, how they conveyed the feelings that they hadn't yet put into words. Did he love her? He wasn't sure. But was he falling in love with her? There was a very good possibility he was.

"Books," she murmured when he finally drew away. "You have to stop distracting me."

"All right," he whispered. "Let's get your books. We'll continue this later."

As Danny followed her around the bookstore, pointing out volumes that belonged in her library, he thought about the time they had left together. He had at least another two weeks of work to do and he could maybe stretch it into three. But her work in Ireland would eventually end.

He tried to imagine how that would look, how it would feel. Would they just kiss each other goodbye and end it? Or would they make plans to see each other again? Though he'd always been one to make a break up clean and simple, somehow he knew it wouldn't be simple with Jordan. He was already thinking of ways they could be together, of trips to New York.

He needed time. Or he'd have to make better use of the time he had. Riley had only been given a couple of weeks with Nan. How had he managed it? Maybe it was time to find out.

5

THEY'D PACKED THE CAR with boxes of books, the scent of old leather filling Jordan's station wagon. More books would be delivered to the house tomorrow and the shop-keeper had found additional sets in Dublin and Galway that he'd ordered for Jordan and send on through a de-livery service.

As they drove along the coast, the sun disappeared, replaced by steely-gray clouds and a soft drizzle. Jordan stared out the window as she listened to the gentle rhythm of the wipers.

Even on such a dreary afternoon, the countryside still looked so green and magical. Until Danny had come into her life, she'd been immune to its charms. But now, caught in an affair with a sexy Irishman, she could appreciate the place that had made him.

There was something about the light, how it shim-mered over the landscape, intensifying the colors and the contrasts: soft green moss growing on weathered gray rock, white clouds blowing above the deep blue of the Atlantic. Ireland was alive.

Was it the land or was it the man she was with? Had

Danny made her more aware of her surroundings? Her senses were so much more heightened now. Smells and tastes could elicit an overwhelming pleasure for her. Back home, there was a quiet sameness to all her days and nights, as if she were just wandering from one day to the next, waiting for something important to happen.

Now it had. She glanced over at him, then reached out and ran her hand through his hair, brushing a stubborn curl away from his face.

"What?" he said, looking over at her.

"Nothing," Jordan replied. "I just felt like touching you."

Danny smiled. "I know how you feel. I pretty much think about touching you all the time."

"I know," Jordan said.

"You do? How do you know?"

"I just do." She looked out the window at the landscape passing by. "I love Ireland. I didn't think I would, but I do. Even in the rain, it's beautiful." She paused. "Have you ever thought of leaving?"

Danny shook his head. "No. Maybe for a holiday. I could imagine living in another country for a year or two. But I'd have to come back. Some of my cousins live in America," he said. "In Boston. And I have cousins in New York and California, too. But I've never met them."

"I feel like I haven't really seen a lot of the country. I've been to almost every antique store, but I haven't been to Blarney Castle."

"Blarney Castle is for the tourists. We'll go to the Burren and the Cliffs of Moher. We'll see the natural sites, not the ones with lines of tourists."

"What else will you show me?" Jordan asked.

"There is a place I could show you right now," Danny said. "I think you'll like it. And it's on the way to Ballykirk."

"It's raining," she said.

"Even better," he replied. "We may see something interesting in the rain."

"Is it a stone circle? I went to visit a stone circle here. I thought it would be like Stonehenge, but it was really small."

"Our stone circles aren't nearly as grand. But they're populated by much more interesting spirits."

"So, where are we going? Is it on my map?"

"I'm not going to tell you," he said.

"Will it have a gift shop?"

Danny chuckled. "No. No gift shop."

Jordan continued to question him, making a game of it, trying to tease the answer out of him. Danny grabbed her hand and laced his fingers through hers. "Look how happy you are when we're out of that house," he said. "We need to make a point of getting away more often. You never look like this when you're sitting in your office, worrying over your reports."

"How do I look when I'm in my office?"

He pulled a silly face and Jordan couldn't help but laugh. "I look constipated?"

"That was cheesed off," Danny said. "You look annoyed. As if you'd rather be doing anything else."

"And how do I look when I'm in bed with you?"

He made another face, his eyes fluttering and his lips parted.

"Drunk," she said. "You're not very good at faces."

Danny navigated the station wagon through brilliant green hillsides along the coast. At a rocky pass, they waited for a herd of sheep to cross the road and when they wouldn't move, Danny jumped out of the car and helped the farmer hurry them along.

No matter where she looked, there was something beautiful to see—a thatch-roofed cottage, an old cemetery filled with ornate Celtic crosses, the ruin of an ancient church.

They passed a number of signs for tourist attractions, but Danny continued on. Then he turned off the main road onto a narrow lane. Drystone walls lined either side of the road and bushes arched above them until they were driving through a tunnel of thick greenery. They came out on the other side and he pulled the car into a small parking spot, cut into the stone fence.

"This is it," he said, hopping out of the driver's side. He reached in the backseat and grabbed his jacket, then hurried around to help her out. They found a muddy footpath leading through a grove of trees.

The drizzle had turned to a light mist and Jordan pulled her jacket more tightly around her. Danny held the umbrella over her head, helping her over rocky spots along the path. And then he stopped. "This is it," he murmured.

Jordan glanced around. There wasn't much to see. They stood in the middle of some sort of circle, the earth mounded up with trees planted on either side of the small ridge. The entire circle was no more than forty or fifty feet in diameter. "What is this place?"

"This is a fairy circle," Danny said.

"It looks like a little shallow in the woods. Maybe there was a pond here at one time."

"No, it's a fairy circle. They're all over Ireland. Sometimes you find them in the middle of a meadow, just a ring of mushrooms. Or they can be made of stones. The farmers won't touch them for fear of grievous bad luck."

"Where are the fairies?"

"They're watching us. You should be able to see them, *sidhe*."

"I'm not a fairy."

"That's what a fairy would say."

Jordan slowly walked along the elevated ridge, careful not to trip on the exposed roots from the trees. "How did this happen?"

"They say the fairies dance round and round in a circle and the earth rises up beneath them. If you walk around the circle and make a wish, it will come true."

"I don't believe that," Jordan said. "Someone piled up the dirt in a circle."

"They also say, if a man finds himself alone in a fairy ring with a fairy, then he belongs to her forever." Danny took her into the center of the ring, then stood behind her, lifting her arms up to the sky. "Close your eyes," he whispered.

Jordan did as she was told. Without sight, her hearing became more acute. At first, she thought it was merely the wind whistling through the trees, but then she began to hear singing. Soft, sweet voices on the breeze. "I hear them," she said, opening her eyes and searching the landscape.

The magic was all around them, like electricity in the

air. "I feel their presence," she said. Slowly she turned, searching the trees for a sight of them.

"I told you. You have fairy blood coursing in your veins. *Leanan sidhe.* She chooses a human to love and if the human doesn't love her, she becomes his slave. But if he does love her, then he is hers, forever. But forever isn't very long, because the lovers of the *leanan sidhe* always die young. They say that's why so many Irish writers and poets and artists die young, because they are captivated by the *leanan sidhe.*"

"I'm not going to kill you," Jordan said.

Danny reached out and smoothed his hand over her cheek, tucking a windswept strand behind her ear. "I know. But sometimes it feels that way."

Jordan closed her eyes and turned into his touch, waiting for him to kiss her. When he finally did, his mouth was warm and demanding.

"Like now," he whispered. "I feel like I'm going to die if I can't have you."

Jordan parted her lips as the kiss deepened and she felt her mind spinning with desire and her body pulsing with wild sensations. The kiss ended slowly, Danny nuzzling his face into the curve of her neck.

"You have bewitched me," he said.

"And can you escape from the *leanan sidhe?*"

"Only if I find someone to take my place," he said. "Another man to capture your fancy."

"I don't want anyone but you," Jordan whispered back.

The wind freshened and her hair whipped around her face. Danny glanced up at the sky. "It looks like it's going to rain again."

Jordan laughed as a big droplet hit her face. "You do weave a good tale, Danny Quinn. You almost had me convinced."

"How do you explain it then?" He took her hand and pressed it to his chest. "I can't resist you. All I think about, day and night, is touching you, kissing you." He wrapped his arms around her waist.

"If you really think I'm going to lead you to an early death then you'd better run away right now. Get out of this fairy ring."

"I'm not going anywhere," he said.

She chuckled. "I wonder why we don't have any mythological creatures in the States? We have ghosts. But you have fairies and leprechauns and trolls and dragons."

Danny grabbed her by the waist and drew her over to one of the trees, trapping her against it with his arms. He pressed his hips against hers and stared down into her eyes. "Can you feel it?" he murmured, his hands skimming over her damp clothes.

"What?" Jordan teased.

His lips were warm against her throat. "Your magic. I can't stop myself. You're too powerful."

Jordan laughed. "I've come to realize that you will use any excuse to get lucky. Are you saying you're under a spell now?"

"I am. And it's your fault. You and your fairy ways."

Jordan shook her head. "You don't seem particularly intent on resisting me." She took his hand and placed it on his chest. "See. It's not as though you can't control yourself."

He moved his hand back to her breast. "It does that

all on its own. I can't control it." He reached down and slipped his hand beneath her shirt, finding the warm skin beneath.

Jordan shivered at his touch, then mimicked his caress, slipping her hand under his jacket and sliding her palm up his chest. "Oh, no. I think it's contagious. Maybe we should get out of here before something else starts acting up on its own." She glanced down at the front of his jeans. "Oh dear, I think it might be too late."

He cupped her breast in his palm and ran his thumb over her nipple, drawing it to a peak. Jordan sighed softly and closed her eyes and a moment later, his lips met hers in a deep, demanding kiss.

Suddenly, the skies opened above them and the rain came down in sheets. Jordan yelped and Danny grabbed her hand and they ran back to the car. By the time they jumped inside they were both soaked to the skin.

He pulled her across the console to continue what they'd begun outside. Jordan couldn't stop touching him. Her hands shoved his T-shirt up, revealing the hard flesh of his belly. Impatient, Danny twisted out of his jacket, then yanked the T-shirt over his head.

The heat from their bodies fogged the windows and the sound of the rain on the roof was a counterpoint to their soft moans and sighs. Jordan pressed her lips to his chest. She was still fully clothed and he'd made no move to undress her, his hand still hidden beneath her shirt.

Slowly, she drew her tongue along his chest to his nipple, then circled it several times. It grew to a hard peak in the chill and Jordan continued to tease at it. He groaned softly, and ran his fingers through her hair, tangling in the rain-soaked strands.

Her hands drifted down to his belt and then lower, smoothing over the fabric of his jeans until she felt his erection beneath. Normally, she might have hesitated outside the privacy of the manor house. But they were all alone in the woods and the fairy circle had worked its magic.

Danny watched as she fumbled with the button of his jeans, holding his breath as if her touch were enough to send him over the edge. She glanced up to see him smiling, droplets still clinging to his thick dark lashes.

"I guess the fairies have spoken," he said.

Jordan slipped her hand inside his boxers, wrapping her fingers around his hard shaft. "I suppose we ought to listen to them."

"I've always wanted to make love in the rain. And we have this place all to ourselves. We could take our clothes off and lie down in the grass."

"What if someone comes along?" Jordan asked.

"They'll think we're fairies," he whispered, touching his lips to hers.

Jordan had never done anything so sexually spontaneous…except for almost everything she'd done with Danny. And what harm could it do? No one could see the spot from the road and there'd be no visitors in the pouring rain.

She wanted to try everything and anything with Danny. "All right," she murmured. Jordan began to shed her clothes and Danny watched, a look of astonishment on his face. When she was completely naked, she turned and looked at him. "Well? What about you?"

"You really want to do this?"

Jordan nodded. "When in Ireland do as the fairies do."

Jordan jumped out of the car, into the downpour. Though the air was cold, the rain felt warm on her skin. She ran, her bare feet slipping on the wet grass, until she stood in the middle of the fairy circle. Then she turned her face up to the sky, reveling in the utter and complete freedom she felt.

Danny joined her a moment later, completely naked and fully aroused. They met in the center of the circle with another kiss, this one deep and stirring, a prelude to the passion they were about to share.

They tumbled down into the soft grass, their limbs tangled together. Jordan had never felt anything like it. It was so completely natural to touch him like this. He rolled her over beneath him, his hips resting between her thighs. "We don't have a condom," he said, cursing softly.

"We don't need one," Jordan replied, pulling him into another kiss.

"Are you sure?"

She nodded. She'd always been careful about birth control, never leaving it to the moment when it was needed. And she was glad that there would be no barriers between them this time. He pulled her thighs against his hips and entered her in one smooth motion, taking her breath away.

He buried himself so completely that Jordan wasn't sure she could take anymore. Danny gazed down into her eyes, smoothing the rain from her face with his hands and kissing her softly. The air around them was alive with electricity, the leaves of the trees rustling overhead.

Slowly, he began to move above her, his gaze still fixed on hers. Jordan could see every moment of pleasure etched across his handsome face, every surge of desire and every determined denial. He drove himself close, then retreated and waited for her, moving against her until he felt her release coming.

Here, in this spot, there was nothing but her desire. The outside world didn't exist, the problems of the day had disappeared, everything in her life had been reduced to this perfect joining. He withdrew and slid against her, teasing at the damp folds until Jordan cried out beneath him.

And then he was inside her again, taking her over the edge, the spasms enveloping her body until she couldn't think any longer. Everything had become sensation: pure, powerful pleasure that raced through her body like a current.

A moment later, he dissolved into his own orgasm, his body driving into hers one last time before he lost control. She whispered his name, urging him on until he was completely sated.

With a sigh, Danny pulled her on top of him, their bodies still joined. He stared up into the sky, the rain splattering in his face. "We have to be gone in the head to be out here in this rain."

"I love it," Jordan said. "I'm not even cold."

"I'm freezing," he said. "And I have grass in places I won't even mention."

A low rumble sounded in the distance. At first,

Jordan thought it was thunder, then realized it sounded more like a car. "Someone's coming."

Danny shook his head. "It's just a car passing by on the road. They won't come out in the rain."

Jordan got to her feet and raked her hands through her hair, letting the deluge wash all the dirt from her naked body. Danny watched her, an appreciative smile on her face. "You are a mysterious creature," he said.

She began to dance, swaying slowly from side to side and—

"Don't worry, Mildred, it's supposed to be here somewhere. A little rain won't hurt ya. Come along now. Step lively."

Jordan spun around to see an elderly couple, decked out in rain gear, stepping into the grove. A tiny scream slipped from her lips and she looked down at Danny. He was already leaping to his feet.

He grabbed her hand and they ran for the car, but not before the couple caught sight of them. Jordan slipped once and Danny steadied her before racing on.

"Look, Mildred, I told you we'd see fairies. Didn't I tell you?"

"Freddie, those are no more fairies than you and I are. Fairies don't drive around the countryside in a Volvo."

Laughing, Jordan and Danny jumped in the car and quickly made their escape. As they swerved down the narrow lane, the car spitting up mud as it gained speed, Jordan pressed her hand to her heart, the laughter making her breathless and dizzy.

They'd made love in a warm, soft bed, on the sofa in the library, on the worktable in the kitchen. But it all seemed so ordinary, so controlled, compared to what they'd just done. Never in her life had she completely surrendered to her desires—until now.

"Are we going to drive all the way home stark naked?" Danny asked. "Or would you like to stop and get dressed?"

She glanced over at him. "Oh, let's have some fun. Forget the clothes."

"You're a woman after my own heart, Jordan Kennally. You know that, don't you?"

I hope so, Jordan said to herself. Because she wouldn't be satisfied with anything less.

"I'M LOSING MY MIND!"

Danny heard Jordan's shout from the breakfast nook, where he was replacing the hinges on the old wooden door. He frowned, then decided to see what had set her off. No doubt she'd just finished her daily report to her father.

There were times when Danny was ready to hop on a plane, fly across the ocean and beat the shite out of the man who made Jordan's life so miserable. How hard would it be to convince him to let Jordan go? Right now, it seemed as if her father kept her employed simply to torture her.

Parents were supposed to support their children, not torment them. He'd always taken his parents for granted, but after hearing about Jordan's dysfunctional family, it was clear that he needed to be much more appreciative of what he had.

Danny found her standing in front of the bookshelves, staring at the neatly arranged shelves of books. She'd spent most of the previous day unpacking the crates and arranging the volumes in the library. But now, she stood in front of her work, shaking her head.

"What is it?" he asked.

"It's gone," she said. "It was here yesterday and it's gone today. I counted out each of these books, matched them up with the packing lists. The Shakespeare plays have thirty-seven volumes. And now there are thirty-six. There's a spot empty right here, where *A Midsummer Night's Dream* belongs."

"Are you sure?"

"Of course I'm sure. I'm not imagining this. It was here yesterday and now it's gone. The set isn't worth anything if it's incomplete." She turned away from the bookcase and began to pace the room. "We have to get rid of these brownies," she said. "We—we need an exterminator." She reached for the phone book on her desk. "Like those ghostbuster guys in the movie. You have to have someone in Ireland who takes care of these things."

"Of course we do," Danny said. "And they're all scoundrels and cheats. They'll take your money, sprinkle a few herbs around the room and laugh all the way to the bank."

"What am I supposed to do? I didn't mind it at first, but this set cost five hundred pounds. I'm going to have to replace it."

"Unless we found the person who stole it."

"I thought you said brownies stole it."

He closed the phone book and grabbed her hand, leading her along to the leather sofa. "I don't believe in brownies any more than you do. We need to figure out how this person—and I do believe it's a person—is getting into the house. Remember Kellan told us about the secret passage? We need to find it before anything else goes missing." Danny sat down, then pulled her into his lap, wrapping his arms around her.

"Okay. So how do we do this?"

"We start by checking out the exterior and the cellars. See if we can find any entrances there. They have to come in from the outside in some way. And it can only happen from the exterior walls or the cellar."

"Contractors have been over every inch of this place," she said. "The cellars are solid stone so that can't be it."

"The pool," Danny said. "What better place to hide an entrance?"

"No. You'd be able to see an entrance down there. The walls are tiled."

"Maybe Kellan is wrong," he murmured.

"No, he has to be right. My question is, who is coming in and why? They really haven't stolen anything of value. They're just causing mischief."

"Maybe it's a kid," Danny said, smoothing a strand of hair from her temple. "Before you started working on this house, it was open for years. Maybe one of the kids who hung out here found the secret entrance and is just coming in out of curiosity."

"That makes sense," Jordan said.

"We need to let the dogs sleep in the house," Danny said. "If someone comes in, they'll bark."

Jordan thought about his suggestion for a moment. She hadn't allowed Finny and Mogue into the house since that very first night, when she'd thought someone was in her room. Danny understood her reluctance, considering all the work that had been done on the wooden floors. But the best defense against a troublemaker was a four-legged offense.

"All right. But I'm going to make them wear those little booties that I make the contractors wear."

"They're not going to like that," Danny said. "Besides, they won't stay on. I'll trim their nails. They'll be fine."

Jordan drew a deep breath. "All right. I feel better. Now that we have a plan, we're going to figure this out."

Danny forced a smile. If only the rest of their troubles were so easy to solve.

He wanted to talk about what was going to happen between them when the job was over. He needed to know where he stood. All the guessing was wearing on him and he'd grown sick of trying to interpret every little thing she said to him.

When they were together, intimately entangled, Danny knew there was something there, something much deeper than just lust. When he moved inside her, it wasn't about his pleasure, it had become all about her, as if the beauty and power of their physical relationship might somehow prove to her they belonged together.

Every day that passed, he saw proof of the end. The painters were gone, the roofers were finished. Books now filled the shelves in the library, utensils and pots and pans hung from the racks in the kitchen, and furniture and rugs would arrive in a few days. After that, the house would be transformed from a construction site to a home and it would all be over.

It was a day that Jordan was anxiously awaiting and one he could only dread. Why was he so afraid to broach the subject with her? Danny suspected that he wasn't ready to hear her answer.

If she was planning to walk away without a second thought, then he didn't want to know until the very last moment of their time together. She had bewitched him, and like the other victims of the *leanan sidhe,* he would pay for his desire when she let him go. Though it wouldn't be death, he might feel like it for a time.

"Why don't we just take a little break?" he suggested, nuzzling her neck. "We could go down and take a swim. Or we could go out and get an early supper."

"We're always taking little breaks from work," Jordan said.

"I don't mean that kind of break," he said, referring to their sexual trysts. "Let's just get out of the house and do something. Take a drive, take a walk. It's a beautiful autumn day and you've been cooped up inside for too long. And I want to spend some time with you. Nothing more."

"I can't leave," she said. "I have all this work to do and I—"

"I'm not asking you to take an ocean voyage for feck's sake," Danny teased.

She shrugged. "I know. But I sort of have something important to do this afternoon and I really wouldn't be very good company. And I need some time to work up my courage."

"Are you planning to go cliff diving? Or will you be jumping out of a plane?"

Jordan giggled. "No, nothing so simple. I'm going to call my father and give him an ultimatum. Either he gives me the hotel job or I'm going to quit."

A gasp slipped from Danny's throat, her statement taking him by surprise. If she wasn't working for her family then she wouldn't be tied to New York anymore. "Are you sure you want to do that?"

"Yes," Jordan said, nodding. "Absolutely. And I have you to thank for that."

"Me?"

"I've always been so careful about everything I've done in my life. Until I met you. Then I just threw caution to wind. I had sex in the middle of a fairy circle yesterday. I was naked, running around in the rain. If I can do that, I can certainly be honest with my father. It's time I stood up to him."

"And what will you do if he gives you the job?" Danny asked.

Jordan opened her mouth to reply, then paused, frowning. "I'll do the job," she murmured. "I'll do a really good job and prove that I'm just as good as any of my brothers."

"And if he refuses?"

She thought about the question for a long moment. "I don't know. I suppose I should figure that out, too." Jordan drew a ragged breath. "I guess I'll…quit."

Danny grabbed her hand and laced his fingers through hers. "Are you really ready to do that?"

"It's always been an option," she said. "I've almost done it a few times in the past, but then talked myself out of it. I can't continue like this, Danny. I should be worth something to him, as a daughter *and* an employee. Maybe it's time to find out where I stand."

"Why do you care what your father thinks? You're an adult. You don't need his approval."

Jordan laughed. "Yeah, right. Don't even try to ana-lyze me. I've spent a lifetime trying to figure out why I seek my father's approval. It's just something I do. My brothers do it also. But I'm just willing to suffer more to get what I want."

"You're suffering?" Danny asked.

"Well, not at the moment."

"I bet your brothers never had sex with one of their employees," he said. "That's wicked suffering there."

"You're not my employee and I'm not your boss, re-member?"

He grabbed her waist and set her on her feet, then stood beside her. "Give me a half hour."

"For what?"

"A swim. We could get naked, play in the water, have a little fun and have you back at work before anyone knows you're missing."

"You just want to get my clothes off," she said.

"Yes, I do. That is pretty much my goal from the time we get up in the morning until the time we crawl into bed at night."

"Oh, so now I get the real story. You're not interested in making gates and medallions and hinges anymore. This is all about me and you."

"Now you're starting to understand. Finally. It's about bloody time." He reached for the hem of her shirt. "I'll race you. First one naked and in the water wins."

Jordan slowly shook her head. "No, no, no."

"Yes, yes, yes," he said, tugging his T-shirt over his head. He watched as her gaze drifted over his chest, then reached for the button of his jeans. He unzipped them and skimmed them down his hips, kicking off his shoes before casting the jeans aside.

He was left in only his boxers and when he hooked his fingers in the waistband, Jordan sucked in a sharp breath. With deliberate ease, he slowly slid them down until he was standing in front of her, completely naked.

"All right," she finally said. "It would probably be better to call my father tomorrow. He's always in a bad mood on Tuesdays."

"That's my girl," Danny said. "Since I've had a head start, I'll let you catch up before we race to the pool."

"Here?"

Danny nodded. "Yes."

Jordan took the opportunity to perform a very sexy striptease for him and when she had him completely distracted with her naked body, took off for the door. Danny headed to the kitchen and the stairs that led down from there, but Jordan took the opposite path, taking the stairs near the front door. By the time he reached the pool, she was already treading water in the deep end.

"You have a half hour," she called, her voice echoing against the tiles. "You'd better make it worth my time."

IT WAS NEARLY 9:00 p.m. when Jordan pulled up in front of the manor house. The drive back and forth to Wexford was a long one, but her time had gone to a good cause. Over the past sixteen months, she'd visited hundreds of antique stores all over Ireland. To her delight, she'd found period fixtures for almost every room in the manor house. Today had brought a small chandelier for the upper hallway.

The only problem with a day away was that she hadn't had her regular dose of Danny Quinn. She'd grown used to seeing him whenever the impulse stuck.

But the ride to Wexford had given her time to think about all that had happened since his arrival at Castle Cnoc. Though she'd vowed to keep their relationship simple, the deeper her affections grew, the more difficult it became. She found herself fantasizing about a real future with the sexy Irishman.

She imagined them strolling the streets of Manhattan together, buying a weekend house in Connecticut, keeping an apartment in the city, enjoying everything that New York had to offer. Other times, she imagined herself living here in Ireland, raising a family and making a home with him. But always, she came to the realization that if they were to have a future, one of them would have to sacrifice.

Though she'd been determined to call her father and give him her ultimatum, Jordan had been putting it off for the past few days. Tomorrow was Friday and after that, the weekend. She'd call him at home on Sunday morning, knowing that without the pressures of the office, he might be more amenable. Plus, her mother would be there to run interference.

In truth, she was afraid of his answer. If he did allow her to quit, then she had to decide what to do with the rest of her life. At least now, everything was still in limbo. She still had choices.

As she stepped out of the car, she saw Danny standing at the front door. The scaffolding was gone and the original door was hung with brand-new hinges and hardware. Progress, she mused. That always brought a smile to her face.

"Hey, baby," he said with a devilish smile. "Welcome home."

"You've been busy," she said. "It looks incredible." He swung the door back and forth on its hinges, demonstrating how smoothly it worked. "Very nice job. Have you been waiting here long?"

"All afternoon. But I have a good reason," he said.

"You always have a good reason," she teased.

He strode up to her and picked her up off her feet, wrapping her legs around his waist. "I'm not always thinking about sex," he said. "I have other things going on in my life."

"Like what?"

Danny carried her into the house. But instead of heading back to the office, he carried her up the stairs, his mouth warm on her throat. They walked to her bedroom and then into the bathroom.

"What are we doing?"

"I'm going to draw a bath for you and then you're going to relax and tell me about your day. And then I'm going to ask you something and you're going to say yes."

"Don't I always say yes?"

"That's true. And after you say yes, we're going to have some dinner and spend the rest of the night in bed."

She slipped out of her jacket and tossed it aside, then rubbed her stiff neck. Hours in the car had exhausted her and she couldn't think of anything she wanted more than a hot bath. But her curiosity was piqued. What was he going to ask? she wondered. What was so important to him that he'd bribe her with a bath to get a positive response?

"Ask me now," Jordan demanded.

"It can wait," he said.

As the water ran into the huge clawfoot tub, Danny slowly undressed her. When she was naked, he stood back and stared at her. It felt odd for him to be fully clothed while she was naked. Not odd, she thought. Erotic. "No, I want to know now. Did you go over budget? Did you mess something up?"

"It's not about the house." He helped her into the tub, then handed her a glass of wine that he'd set on the floor.

"What is it?" she asked, sinking down into the hot water. "I want to know."

He cursed softly. "This is supposed to be relaxing and now you're all tense," he said. "It's really nothing."

"If it's nothing, than you can ask me now. Do you need a day off? Is that it?"

He reached into the back pocket of his jeans and handed her an envelope. "It's an invitation to my gallery opening on Saturday night. I'm showing a couple of pieces and I thought you might like to come with me. As my date."

Jordan stared at the invitation, warmed by his offer. "Yes," she murmured. "Yes, I'd love to go as your date."

He seemed pleased with her answer, dropping a quick kiss on her shoulder. "It's in Dublin. I thought we could go and spend the night. Maybe see a bit of the city on Sunday. Make a weekend out of it."

Though Jordan had never spent more than a day away from Castle Cnoc, she realized that time with Danny was running out. There were so many things she wanted to experience with him, but every day that passed was one less she'd have with him. By her estimate, they had less than a month left. And yet, any time spent in Danny's company was better than her solitary life in New York.

Was he really what she'd been waiting for? This wasn't supposed to be how it happened. She wasn't supposed to fall in love with an Irish blacksmith with thick, dark hair and bottomless blue eyes.

She opened her eyes and glanced at him. Danny wasn't pretty, he was sheer masculine perfection. He wore his looks the way he wore his clothes, casually, as if he weren't aware of the effect they had on her. She was so accustomed to neatly tailored men that he seemed exotic and forbidden.

"In Manhattan, gallery openings are pretty fancy affairs. Are they that way in Dublin?"

He chuckled. "You're going to see me in a proper jacket," he said. "No tie, but I'm going to look very sexy. The women will be all over me."

"I didn't ask so you could tell me about your wardrobe choice. I'll need to decide on a dress."

"I could take you shopping," he said.

"I have the perfect dress at home. I'll have it sent from New York this afternoon."

"Then it's all settled. On Saturday, we're going to Dublin." He was watching her through hooded eyes. "Now, tell me about your day."

"Chandelier for the upper hallway, monogrammed towels for the bathrooms, still looking for decent sheets. May have to do mail order from Frette. Unless I take a weekend and go to Italy for linens. Or Paris."

"Is that even a possibility?"

"Yes," Jordan said. "If that's what's needed, that's what I'll do. I'd prefer to stick with Irish linens though. Maybe if we left tonight, I could shop tomorrow in Dublin." She groaned softly and leaned back in the bath. "God, I'm so sick of shopping." She glanced over at him. "Enough about me. What did you do all day long?"

"Thought about you in the bed," he said. "Made some hinges. Thought about you in the bathtub. Worked on the garden gate. Thought about you in the swimming pool, designed a front gate for the drive."

"Really?" She laughed. "So, you had a productive day."

"Yes," he said. "So, boss, give me a job to do. I could rub your feet. Or wash your back. Or massage your shoulders."

"All of those would be nice," she murmured.

"I'll start with the shoulders." He sat down behind her and began to knead the knotted muscles. She tipped her head to the side and he pressed his lips to a spot at the base of her neck. "Do you ever wonder what you'd be doing if you hadn't come here to Castle Cnoc?" she asked.

"What do you mean?"

"Our lives seem so intertwined here. What if you were alone? What would you be doing right now?"

"I'd probably be sitting at the pub, having a beer with my brothers. Maybe tending the bar, drawing Guinness. Then a game of darts or billiards." He chuckled. "Jaysus, I had a boring life before I met you."

"Me, too," she said. "I spent my free time searching the internet for fabric and furniture and fixtures. The highlight of my evening would be my decision whether to have a ham sandwich or a grilled cheese. Dinner would be followed by whatever bestseller I was reading."

"I'd say we were damn lucky to meet each other."

"You've ruined me for other men, you know."

"How is that?"

"The sex. It's too good."

He rested his chin on her shoulder. "How can the sex be too good?"

"I never really thought sex was important," Jordan admitted. "My parents aren't very loving with each other. Our family shows affection by insulting each other. We just weren't…physical. But with you, we always seem to be touching."

"I like that," Danny said.

"Me, too. And I never thought I would. I'd sit in the subway or at the park and watch couples hanging all over each other and wonder why they couldn't contain themselves. Now I understand." She turned and kissed his cheek. "Just the tiniest thing can bring the biggest thrill."

He smoothed his palms over her shoulders and chest, then cupped her breasts. "You do have a very touchable body, boss."

Jordan moaned softly as his thumbs rubbed across her nipples. She'd grown accustomed to this power that she held over him. When he touched her, she didn't feel like a boss or Andrew Kennally's daughter or the Kennally brothers' younger sister or Kencor's "decorator." She was just a woman.

Her heart slammed in her chest and she arched to

meet his caress. Danny circled the tub and pulled her to her feet, wrapping his arms around her naked body as his lips captured hers.

Jordan was always amazed at how powerful his kiss was. He was able to take her breath away, to make her body ache, to send her heart racing, by simply covering her mouth with his. He had a way of possessing her that made her feel weak and powerful all at once.

The kiss spun out in one long, delicious encounter, growing deeper and more passionate with every breath they shared. Danny's hands smoothed over her damp skin but Jordan's touch was hampered by his clothes.

A frustrated moan slipped from her throat as she fumbled with the buttons of his shirt. She needed him naked, needed his skin touching hers. "Stop." Pressing her hands to his chest she pushed him back. "Take off your clothes."

"No," he said.

Jordan frowned, shaking her head. "No?"

"No," Danny said. "If I take off my clothes, then I'm not going to be able to stop myself. I think we should just take our time. We have the whole evening."

"Am I the boss or are you?"

"You're the boss," he said.

"Then you're supposed to follow my orders?"

"Yes, ma'am."

"Take off your clothes, Danny Quinn. And make it snappy."

With a reluctant smile, he slowly stripped. When his boxers were around his feet, he braced his hands on his hips. "Now what? Would you like me to fix that squeaky hinge or change the oil in your car?"

"Get in the tub," Jordan ordered.

He did as he was told, sliding down into the warm water. Then Jordan climbed in and straddled his waist, his hard shaft pressing against the crease between her legs. She grabbed a sponge and lathered it up then ran it over his chest.

"Isn't this considered sexual harassment?"

"Yes," she said. "And I could get fired for this."

"Really?"

Jordan nodded. "Really. But you're not going to say anything, are you?"

"Never," he said. "As long as you promise to keep harassing me, I'll keep quiet."

She leaned over and kissed him and when she moved back, Jordan shifted on top of him, slowly taking him inside her. A gasp slipped from her lips and she smiled. "I think we're going to be getting into a little overtime tonight."

"I'm ready to do whatever it takes to get the job done."

6

DANNY AND JORDAN ARRIVED in Dublin by mid-afternoon on Saturday. Danny insisted on driving Jordan's Volvo, making it from County Cork to Dublin in record time. As they raced over the curving highways, he felt as if they were setting off on a grand adventure, even though it was only a night in the city.

They weren't boss and employee now. They were a couple having a little holiday together. She was his lover, his girlfriend, his date. And it felt good to be like everyone else in the world. Just two people falling in love.

They did some shopping for linens, then checked into a room at a nice hotel. Though Jordan tried to insist on paying for it, expensing it along with the sheets, Danny refused. He wanted the weekend to be his treat and Jordan reluctantly accepted. In truth, he had all sorts of things he wanted to show her.

They got dressed for the opening, then went out for a stroll before dinner. O'Connell Street was famous for its shops, but Danny had decided to take Jordan on a sculpture tour. They began with the statue of James

Joyce and then moved on to Daniel O'Connell. James Larkin was next. The last sculpture was inside an imposing building.

"I used to come here all the time when I was at university," Danny said, holding the door open for her. "It's a pretty special place in my family history."

"What is this, a museum?"

"No," Danny said. "It's the post office."

"You spent time at the post office?"

Danny nodded. "I know. It's a bit strange, but I'll explain." They stood in the center of the lobby, Danny holding tight to her hand. "This is where the rebellion began. This is where my great-great-grandfather on my mother's side made his stand against the British soldiers. The Easter Uprising was kind of like your revolution." He pointed to the statue. "That's Cuchulainn."

"Did he fight in the rebellion?" Jordan asked.

Danny shook his head. "No, he's one of our mythological heroes. His big victory was the cattle raid of Cooley."

"He stole cows?"

"No, he protected the bull of Ulster from Queen Maeve's soldiers."

"He protected a cow—"

"A bull. *The* bull."

"And he gets a statue."

"I guess he's a martyr to cattle protection. Queen Maeve set her sorcerers on him and killed him after he saved the bull. The statue is in memory of the fourteen rebels that were executed after the Easter Uprising."

"That makes much more sense," Jordan said.

They stared up at the statue for a long time before

Jordan slipped her arms around Danny's waist and gave him a hug. "I like it. I think it's the nicest one we've seen tonight. Except for yours, of course."

"You are not required to like my work," Danny said. "The sculptures you're going to see tonight are pretty abstract."

"I'm going to love your work," she said. "I know I will."

They strolled out onto the street. There was a chill in the air and Danny slipped out of his jacket and draped it around Jordan's shoulders. "Have I told you how beautiful you look in that dress?" he asked.

"Yes. Lots of times. At least twenty since I put it on at the hotel."

"Well, then this is twenty-one. You do look incredible. You're going to be the most beautiful woman in the room tonight."

"And you're required to say that," she teased.

"No," Danny replied, shaking his head. "That's the thing about you. You don't have any idea how pretty you are. I think you've spent so much time trying to be one of the guys that you don't have any sense of who you are as a woman."

"I did feel that way," Jordan said, stunned that he'd sensed it. "You make me feel…feminine." She held up the sleeve of his jacket. "Like this. My brothers would never think to offer me a jacket if I was cold. They'd just yell at me for forgetting to bring my own along. And they'd never tell me I was pretty. They'd just make some stupid comment about my pigeon-toes or my knobby knees. Or they'd start in on my chest."

"They make fun of your chest?"

"It's often the topic around the Thanksgiving table. They think that teasing me is great family fun. I take a lot of abuse for being the only girl. Especially when my father encourages it."

Danny frowned. "Next time you have a family dinner, you call me. I'll come and stand up for you. I'm pretty good with my fists and I'm the master of the verbal put-down. Your brothers wouldn't pick on you again. Truth told, my two brothers and I could best your four brothers in a good scrap."

"That's not the worst of it. My mother tells me if I'd just get married and bring a husband home, my brothers would show me more respect." Jordan paused. "Not that I'd expect you to marry me. It—it's just what my mother said."

"Do you ever think about getting married?"

"Sure. I think every woman does. But it's not something that I'm focused on. What about you?" It was the truth. Since meeting Danny she had thought about it more than she had before; but it still didn't mean that she wanted to marry him. That would require a complete shift in her priorities.

"I don't really think about it either," Danny said. "But it's a possibility. My brother Riley met Nan and now they're going to get married and that was just this last summer." He shook his head. "It's a strange thing. A wee bit frightening. That things can change so quickly and there's nothing to be done about it."

"Marriage just hasn't fit into my plans."

"Mine neither," Danny said. *Not that it couldn't,* he thought. But he wasn't ready to say that out loud.

A long silence grew between them as they walked

down the sidewalk to the restaurant. He hadn't felt so uncomfortable around Jordan since the day they'd met. Everything had come so easily these past weeks. But maybe this was a conversation that was unavoidable. How much longer could they go on ignoring the future? Sooner or later, they'd have to talk about it.

"You should come to New York sometime," Jordan said. "We have a lot of statues and sculptures there."

"You've got the big one," he said.

"The big one?"

"The Statue of Liberty. That's one thing I'd really like to see."

"Then you'll have to come," she said. It was the closest they'd come to talking about a future together. And Danny was pleased. At least there was a possibility they'd see each other again after she left Ireland.

"What else would we see, besides the inside of your flat?" he asked.

"Depends on when you come. If you come in the fall, we'd go to Central Park. At Christmas, we'd look at the windows at Bloomie's. In the winter, there's skating at Rockefeller Center. In the spring there's baseball at Yankee Stadium. And summer is weekends in the Hamptons. And then we'd eat hot dogs and visit museums and go to Chinatown for Szechuan. We'd take a carriage ride at midnight and go to the top of the Empire State Building and have corned beef sandwiches at the Stage Door Deli and see a Broadway show."

"Jaysus, I can see why you'd want to go home. Ireland must seem like such a bore to you."

"No," she said. "I love Ireland. I didn't at first, but I

think I'm going to miss it after I leave. Who knows, I may come back for visit or two."

Danny chuckled. "I'd like that. Maybe you could find another house to fix up. Kellan's always doing that. You could do another project with him."

"Actually, Kellan talked to me about that. He offered me a job."

Gobsmacked, Danny wasn't sure what to say. Why hadn't she told him this? Why hadn't Kellan mentioned it? Was there a reason they'd keep it a secret from him? "Yeah," he murmured, maintaining an even tone. "That would be really nice."

"But, I think if I come back, I'd want to spend my time seeing Ireland first," she said. "Take some time off. Do a little trip around the country. Like your parents do. What is that called?"

"Caravanning," Danny replied. "So it's good we talked about this. I certainly feel better."

"I do too," Jordan said.

It wasn't much, but Danny did feel relieved. They'd defined their relationship a bit. They'd become so close it had been hard to believe that they'd go their separate ways and never see each other again. Now, they wouldn't.

"And we can always Skype," Jordan said.

"I don't know what that is, but it sounds like fun. Can we do it tonight? And does it involve taking off your clothes?"

"Sometimes it does involve the removal of clothing," Jordan said. "We'll talk about that later."

"Are you hungry? We can eat or we can stop by the

gallery." He pointed across the street. "It's just there. It won't be busy and they always serve finger food."

"Let's go now," Jordan said. "We can always eat later."

He took her hand and they crossed the street, then stopped short before opening the door for her. "What's wrong?" Jordan asked.

"I'm a bit nervous," he said.

"People will love your work," Jordan said.

"I'm not worried about people," Danny said, "I'm worried about you. You're the only one who matters."

He pulled her close and kissed the top of her head. And there it was. No truer words had ever been spoken. If he'd thought he could keep himself from loving Jordan, then he was sadly mistaken. It had already happened. And there was no going back.

BY THE TIME the show officially began, the gallery was packed with guests and press. Jordan had been to a number of openings in Manhattan and this was no different. There was excitement in the air and everyone milled around the pieces, wineglasses dangling from their hands.

Danny stood between his two sculptures, talking to interested guests while Jordan stood nearby, sipping her wine. He seemed like a different person in this environment, so composed and serious, not at all like the funny, teasing man she'd come to know. The suit made him look older, more respectable, and, even though he hadn't combed his hair, he was still dangerously attractive.

As expected, Jordan fell in love with the sculptures

the moment she saw them. He'd told her they were abstract, but there was something about them that brought to mind birds soaring on the air currents over the cliffs near the manor.

The sculptures had been made of copper, the thin sheets bent and crumpled and assembled to create a sense of motion. She could imagine the pieces in a museum or a private home or even the lobby of a public building. Considering the number of people gathered around Danny, Jordan felt confident that the sculptures would be sold before the night was through.

"What do you think?"

Jordan turned to find a woman standing next to her. She was about the same age as Jordan, and dressed entirely in black, her hair cropped short and trendy glasses perched on her nose.

"Sally McClary. I'm the art critic for the *Evening Post*. You seem to be captivated by his work."

"Oh, I am," Jordan said. "I think it's extraordinary."

Sally nodded. "Yes, he is, isn't he."

"Oh, I thought we were talking about his work."

"I am," Sally said. "Not his art work, although that's quite extraordinary, too."

Jordan frowned. What was this woman getting at? What other work did— "Oh, you've seen his commercial work? He's an excellent blacksmith."

"Oh, goodness, no. I'm talking about the man. The gorgeous man beneath those clothes." She took a slow sip of her wine. "He's like a fine work of art himself. Strip the clothes off of him and you could stare at him all day long, couldn't you?" She smiled slyly. "A pity he doesn't spend more time in Dublin. He has quite a group of fans here."

Jordan wasn't sure how to respond. She pasted a smile on her face. "So what do you think of the art?"

"Oh, it's fabulous, of course. But then, I've always been a patron. He needs to work more. There's not enough of his work out there to make an impact on the market. And he needs to show outside Ireland. London. New York. Even Los Angeles. Oh, they'd love him there, don't you think?"

Jordan nodded. "Yes, I suppose they would."

"Well, enjoy the rest of the evening," Sally said. "And take a look at the Deirdan etchings. He's the next big thing. Mark my words."

Jordan watched the woman weave her way through the crowds. She stopped and spoke with Danny, resting her hand on his chest as she leaned in close. He smiled and nodded and Jordan wondered at the easy familiarity. Had they been lovers?

She'd never really considered Danny's past. For all she knew, his sex life had begun the moment they met. But that was silly. He'd been seducing girls since high school and even at two or three females a year, that was still a considerable number.

As Sally walked away, he glanced over and caught Jordan's eye. Was that a trace of worry she saw in his face? Jordan watched him over the rim of her wineglass, trying to read his expression. When he excused himself, she gulped down most of her wine, and crossed the room to meet him.

"Are you all right?" he said.

"Sure. Fine," she said. "I was just talking to an art critic. Sally something."

"Right," he said. "Sally McClary. She works for the *Evening Post*. She's a fan."

"I know," Jordan said. "She told me. She seems to be a very devoted fan."

Danny tipped his head as he studied her. "What's that supposed to mean?"

"I don't know. She's the one who started the conversation with me. I got the impression that you two might have been…"

"Did she say that?"

"Not in so many words. Were you?"

He shifted nervously. "Would you be angry if I told you the truth? Because I'll lie if it makes you feel better."

Jordan set her wineglass on the tray of a passing waiter and grabbed another one. "I'm not naive enough to believe you've never been with a woman before me. What you do to me in bed I'm sure comes from lots of experience."

"Not lots," he said. "Well, maybe lots, but that depends upon what you mean by lots."

"You don't need to tell me," Jordan said.

"They don't make any difference," he said. "You're the only woman I want."

"Now," Jordan said.

"Now. Always. Any time." He gave her a seductive smile. "And that sounded really trite, didn't it?" He grabbed her arm and pulled her along to a quiet corner in the gallery.

"This really isn't necessary." Jordan put down her

glass and covered her ears. "I don't need to know. I don't want to know."

"You need to know this," he said. Danny slipped his hands around her waist and pulled her closer. "I'm glad you're here with me tonight. There isn't anyone else I'd rather have here. And I like introducing you as my girlfriend, because that's what you are. And that's important."

"Have you had a lot of girlfriends?" Jordan asked.

"No," he said. "I can count them on one hand. Actually, on three fingers, counting you. And that says something about my feelings for you, Jordan. I think I'm falling for you."

Jordan slowly lowered her hands and took a quick sip of her wine. This was not what she expected. His revelation changed everything. She felt the undeniable urge to run away and glanced around, looking for an escape route.

"No," he said. "You don't have to run. It's all right. I'm just being honest. No harm in that."

"But I—"

He pressed a finger to her lips. "I know. And that's all right." He looked at his watch. "Why don't we get out of here? I've been the accommodating artist for three hours. I think I'm all right to leave."

"I could use some air," she admitted.

Danny said his goodbyes and a few minutes later, they were back on the street, strolling among the crowds of locals and tourists on O'Connell Street. Danny slipped his arm around her shoulders and they walked to the end of the street, to the river. They found a spot near the bridge and Jordan leaned against the railing and stared into the water.

"I shouldn't have said that," Danny murmured.

"No, I'm glad you did," she said. "It's how I feel, too."

"You do?"

"I do. But I don't know what it means. I guess it's not unexpected. We've been spending every minute together for over a month. It would be difficult not to develop feelings for each other."

"Exactly," he said.

"I just don't think we should have too many expectations," she said.

"Expectations." Danny chuckled softly. "That's funny. Maybe it's about time someone expected something from me when it came to romance."

"Can we just enjoy our weekend here and not worry so much about the future?" Jordan asked.

Danny nodded. "Yeah, we can do that. Come on, let's go find a pub, have a pint and enjoy ourselves."

He pulled her into his arms and kissed her, standing beneath a street lamp while the river flowed quietly nearby. For Jordan, it was the most perfect kiss they'd ever shared because it confirmed the words he'd spoken earlier.

He was falling for her. She should have been jumping for joy, shouting to the rooftops that the man she wanted felt the same way about her. But the revelation was bittersweet. It didn't make things simpler. It only made them more difficult.

DANNY GLANCED AT THE CLOCK on the bedside table. It was nearly eleven and he'd made no attempt to crawl out of bed and get the day started. After the show last night, he and Jordan had hit the town, finding a pub near the hotel and spending the night dancing and laughing and having more fun than he'd ever had with a woman.

He loved introducing her to the wonders of Ireland. Last night it was Irish art and Guinness. Today it would be a decent Irish breakfast and a stroll along the Liffey.

He drew a deep breath and closed his eyes, snuggling into her warm, naked body. From the moment he'd met Jordan, there'd been an undeniable attraction between them, a connection that seemed to be strengthened with each moment they spent in bed. They'd been so wrapped up in each other, he'd forgotten that she wasn't completely his.

Was this what Riley had gone through with Nan? His brother had fallen in love with an American tourist with a life and a career in the States. But he'd made it work, he'd convinced her to stay. How had he made that happen?

When they'd begun, Danny was happy just being with Jordan. He'd never thought about anything beyond the next time they found themselves in bed. But somewhere along the line, he'd forgotten about immediate gratification and begun thinking about the future.

She was an incredibly seductive woman. And though she claimed that he was the only one who thought so, Danny suspected the American men she'd known had seen the beauty beneath the businesslike facade. She was his inspiration, his muse, his temptress. Danny couldn't think of anything more he wanted from a woman than what he had with Jordan.

Rolling to his side, Danny wrapped his arm around

her waist and gently brushed a strand of hair from her temple. She sighed softly as he pressed his lips to her forehead. And when his mouth found hers, Jordan stirred and opened her eyes.

"What time is it?" she murmured.

"Almost eleven," he whispered.

Jordan groaned. "Why did you let me sleep so late?"

"It's Sunday. Unless you want to go to church, there isn't much else to do in Dublin. Besides, I kept you up too late last night."

"I'm going to need a vacation from my vacation," she said. "I think I've had more sex in the past month than I've had in my whole entire life. In fact, I'm quite certain of that."

"Well, now there's an accomplishment I can boast about."

"Don't you dare. Your brothers don't need to know about our sex life."

"I'm sure they've already speculated. You don't know what it's like when they get bored at the Hound." He yawned, stretching his arms over his head. "Speaking of the Hound, Riley and Nan's engagement party is coming up. Would you like to go?"

"Wow. Two dates. I don't know," she teased. "Don't you think we're moving a bit fast?"

"Yes," he said, his voice serious. "But I don't have a problem with that. Do you?"

She frowned, staring into his eyes. "No," she said softly. "Are you angry with me?"

"No," Danny said. "I'm just trying to be honest. I don't want to think about you leaving, Jordan. I'm not going to think about it. I'm just going to go on as if we're going to be together as long as we want to be together. Just like any other couple."

"But we aren't any other couple," she said. "I live across the ocean."

"Not now, you don't. Right now, you live in Ireland."

She snuggled closer to his naked body. "Yes, I suppose I do."

"We have the whole day ahead of us. What would you like to do?"

"I'll let you be the tour guide," she said, sliding her hand down his belly. She wrapped her fingers around his shaft, now hard and ready. It always amazed him how quickly that happened with Jordan. All he had to do was think about her and the blood rushed to his crotch.

Danny groaned softly as she began to stroke him, aroused by the prospect of another lazy morning in bed. "I swear to God, you do have fairy blood running through your veins," he murmured. "There's pure magic in the way you touch me."

"Maybe I do," Jordan replied, her touch now playfully teasing. "Since the fairy circle I have been feeling a bit different."

"You're not human," he said, groaning as his pleasure grew. "I'm beginning to believe that I can't live without this." Danny's breath caught in his throat. "I've never been with a woman who makes me feel the way you do."

"I can make you feel even better," she said.

"I'm not sure that's possible," Danny replied.

Jordan slid down along his body, drawing the sheet back, inch by inch. When she reached his waist, she traced a line of kisses across his belly, then moved lower still.

Danny knew what was coming and he wasn't about to stop her. Instead, he stretched his arms over his head and arched his back, waiting for the warmth of her mouth to surround him. When she finally took him between her lips, he was forced to look away. Watching her made it almost impossible to control his release.

There were many things that Jordan was good at, but she excelled at this particular activity. In fact, there were times when he wondered if it could get any better.

But it wasn't just about him. It was about the two of them sharing something so intimate that a touch replaced a word, a sigh replaced a glance. When real life was pushed aside, they had this pleasure between them and it was a powerful drug that he found himself craving constantly.

"Do you know what this does to me?" he whispered.

"Yes," she said. "But isn't that the intended result?"

"No. I'm not talking about an orgasm," he said.

She looked up at him, her hair tumbled around her face, her lips damp. "What?"

"I can't resist you," he murmured. "I don't want to anymore. You've stolen my ability to think for myself."

"That's not true."

He ran his fingers through her hair. "Ask me anything. I'll be your knight in shining armor. I'll slay dragons for you and rescue you from the tower. I'll lay down my life for you. That's what I feel when you touch me."

"Well, the next time I run into a dragon, I'll give you a call," she said, smiling. She moved back to her task, her tongue soft and warm against his shaft.

She thought he was joking. And for a moment, Danny almost let it slide. But he wanted her to understand what she meant to him, how deeply he cared about her. "It's not funny," he said. "I'm tired of dancing around it, playing like it doesn't really matter. You do matter to me, Jordan."

She stared at him. "Don't do this," she murmured. "Don't make it more difficult than it already is."

"I don't give a feck if it is difficult. It should be. It should feel like a knife to the heart, like falling off a cliff onto sharp rocks. It should make your soul bleed. I want it to be hard."

She sat up, pulling the sheet up around her body. "Why? It doesn't have to be."

"It's the only way we're going to know it was real," Danny said.

He reached out and grabbed her waist, then pulled her on top of him. She watched him, warily, all of her insecurities reflected in her expression. He shifted and then he was inside her, in the sweet warmth that had become home to him.

As he moved, Danny felt his need rise, a knot tightening deep inside of him until the ache was too much to bear. He reached between them and touched her, so that he could make her come right along with him.

Danny waited until her face grew flushed with desire, until her breath came in quick, desperate gasps. And then, when he felt her swell around him, he came. The intensity of his release was enough to make his body jerk and his muscles tense. He opened his eyes and watched her dissolve into her own orgasm, her fingers digging into his chest as she rocked above him.

And when she grew still, he pulled her down on top of him, holding her close. "Don't you dare tell me it's going to be easy," he whispered. Danny drew a ragged breath. "I'm going to do everything I can to convince you to stay."

"Please don't do that," Jordan said.

"I don't have any choice."

She fell back asleep stretched out on top of him, her thighs straddling his hips, her head resting on his shoulder. But Danny couldn't sleep. His mind was filled with desperate thoughts.

It was clear she didn't feel the same way about him as he did about her. Every time he brought up the future, she deflected the conversation. He only had two choices—convince her of his point of view or prepare to let her go. But he wasn't going to give up without a fight. He had a chance to change the course of his life, to make Jordan a part of it. And he'd do anything to make that happen.

7

JORDAN CAREFULLY LAID the tape measure down on the floor, measuring the width of the library. She scribbled the number on a pad of paper, then slowly measured in the opposite direction. Kellan had said that if there was a secret entrance into the house, they'd find it this way.

Drawing a ragged breath, she walked out into the foyer. What difference did it make? In a few weeks, the new owners could worry about it. They could afford to hire someone to come in and draw a new floorplan. She glanced down at her watch.

She was already an hour late for Nan and Riley's engagement party and though she was dressed and ready to go, she couldn't bring herself to walk out the front door. Everything was such a mess. The closer she got to finishing, the more confused she became. She'd put off talking to her father for fear that it might force her into a decision she wasn't ready to make. Whenever Danny spoke of the future, she deftly changed the subject. And now, she was quickly losing interest in finally finishing the house.

She pushed the button on the tape measure and it

snapped back into the plastic case. All this indecision was beginning to wear on her. She wanted to know if she had a future at Kencor. She needed to know if she had a future with Danny. It was time to ask the hard questions and get on with the rest of her life.

Jordan grabbed her pad and pencil and strode back to the library. She'd do it now. She'd call her father and if it all went bad, she'd have the party to distract her mind for the rest of the night.

Grabbing her cell phone from the desk, she quickly punched in her father's number and waited as it rang. It was Saturday afternoon in New York. He'd probably be finishing up his regular round of golf at his country club and having a few drinks with his buddies. Now would be a good time. Two martinis always made him more amenable.

The phone rang and then went to voice mail. Drawing a shaky breath, she decided to forgo a message. Maybe it wasn't the right time. But then, a few seconds later, the phone buzzed and she saw an incoming text from her father. "Busy. What do you want?" she read aloud.

"All right. Do it now," Jordan murmured to herself. Ireland job done in two weeks. I want hotel project.

"Matt already started. Maybe next time," she read.

No next time! Hotel project, now, or… Jordan bit her bottom lip, closed her eyes and said a silent prayer. This was the right thing to do. She didn't want to go on working for someone who didn't appreciate her talents.

"Or what?" she murmured.

Was she ready to do this? She was playing a giant game of poker and she was ready to go all in. …I quit. She stared at the words for a long moment, drew another breath and then hit Send. "Oh, God," Jordan groaned. "Please, please, please, let this work. This has to work."

"Hey, what's going on? Why are you still here?"

Jordan jumped at the sound of Danny's voice. She spun around in her chair. "I'm sorry. I just—I had to do this. It couldn't wait."

"What couldn't wait?" Danny asked. "I've been trying to ring you and you haven't answered. I was getting worried."

"I was trying to find the passageway," Jordan lied, grabbing the paper. "I didn't want to leave the house without—"

"The house will be fine. And I promise, we'll look for the passageway tomorrow. I'll help you. It's Sunday, it will be a good way to pass our only day off for the week."

Jordan's phone buzzed and a sick feeling came over her.

"Are you going to answer that?" Danny asked.

She shook her head. "No, not right now." She quickly stood. "I'm ready. Let's go."

Jordan smoothed her hands over the front of her dress, slipping her phone into her skirt pocket, then pasted a smile on her face. Though she'd been looking forward to the party in Ballykirk, right now she felt like crawling into bed and pulling the covers over her head. She'd never held another job. From the moment she was old enough to draw a paycheck from Kencor, she'd worked there.

When they reached the front door, Danny pulled it open, then paused. "Are you all right?"

"Sure. I'm fine." Jordan stopped short. "Wait. I forgot

the gifts. They're on my desk." She turned around and ran back through the foyer and into the library. The two presents had been neatly wrapped earlier that afternoon. But before she picked them up, Jordan pulled her phone from her pocket.

Her throat filled with emotion as she looked at the text. Don't like ultimatums. Finish Cnoc project. Send resignation letter.

That was it, Jordan thought to herself. Just a few sentences and it was over. She waited for the tears, for any reaction. But the only thing she felt was relief. She made her stand, asked for what she wanted and she'd been refused.

"Jordan! What's the holdup?"

She numbly tossed the cell phone on the desk and turned for the door. She'd figure this all out later. Tonight she'd have fun with Danny and his family, drink a bit too much and let him make love to her until nothing mattered but the feel of his body moving inside hers.

When she reached the entryway, she handed him the gifts. "Did you get these?" he asked.

She nodded. "I know it said no gifts on the invitation, but I'm not going to be here for the—" She sighed. "I wasn't going to be here for the wedding, so I wanted to get them something."

"You got them two things?" he asked.

"The smaller is a first-edition Yeats. A collection of his poems. And the other is silver. Hotel silver. It's kind of a trendy thing. You use it for everyday silverware. They're engraved with Qs and Ns and Rs."

"You got them a book and silverware?"

"Yes. I wasn't quite sure which was appropriate so I just bought them both."

"A toaster would have been appropriate."

"But that's so unimaginative," she said. "Everyone buys toasters. I bought something romantic and something useful."

"Should I have gotten a gift?"

"No. The gifts are from the two of us."

As they walked out to the car, Danny gave her hand a squeeze. "I like that," he murmured. "I like that we're a couple."

The pub was packed with barely enough room to move when Danny and Jordan arrived. She stood at his side, clutching his arm and shifting from foot to foot, trying to appear cheerful. A band played on a stage at one end of the pub and a crowd was already on the dance floor, shouting and stomping and clapping. Jordan had been to engagement parties before, but they'd always been very sedate affairs.

The song came to an end and Riley stepped up to the microphone, then pointed directly at them. "It seems my little brother has come back and with a very lovely lass on his arm."

The crowd shouted Danny's name and he chuckled beside her.

"Now, those of you who know Danny know that this is an unusual thing. But I want all of you to give our boyo a good word when you chat with Jordan. She's American and she's beautiful and I don't know what the hell she's doing hanging around my brother, but let's all pretend that he's worth it."

"Hello, Jordan!" the crowd cried out.

Jordan forced a smile and gave them all a weak wave. "Hello," she called. "Nice to be here."

"Kellan, get these two a drink. I'm going to be takin' a break for a few songs so I can go kiss my fiancée," Riley said. "And after that, I've got a special song I want to sing for her."

Kellan had saved seats for them both at the bar and Danny pulled her along through the crowd. She held tight to Danny's hand and was grateful to see a familiar face in Kellan.

"Hello," she said.

"Hi, Joe," Kellen replied with a grin. "What can I get you to drink?"

Jordan glanced around. "A large glass of whatever will get me drunk very quickly. How about one of Nan's margaritas?"

"Forget the fruity drinks," Kellan advised. "Whiskey. A double?"

"Make it a triple."

Kellan poured her a glass, then turned to Danny. "How about you, brother?"

"Nothing for now. I'm driving."

"No, you're not. You're joining in the celebration. And if you have too much, you two can stay up at your place."

"All right, then, give me a pint," Danny said.

Over the next half hour, Jordan was introduced to an endless line of people. She met Danny's parents, Eamon and Maggie Quinn, and his two older sisters and their families. And first cousins and second cousins and third cousins.

Jordan had to wonder where the crowd had come

from. Ballykirk was such a small village. But everyone
in attendance seemed to know the couple quite well,
considering that Nan had only lived in Ireland for a few
months.

This was what family was like, she mused. One big,
happy crowd of people who cared. She'd never really
experienced that before, never even imagined what it
would feel like to be completely comfortable with the
people she was related to.

As the evening went on, the crowd became more and
more boisterous and the music more raucous. This was
the perfect way to distract herself. How could she feel
depressed when faced with Irish pub music? It was all
so cheerful and lively. Danny joined his two brothers
on stage for a set and Jordan found a spot in the shadows to watch them.

"They're a wild bunch."

Jordan glanced to her left to find Nan standing next
to her. "I've never seen him like this," she said. "He
hums while he works, but this is a surprise. I didn't realize he could sing."

Nan gave her a long look. "Are you all right?"

"Yes," Jordan replied. "I'm…I'm fine."

The brothers finally left the stage after a rousing ren-
dition of an Irish reel that left the audience exhausted.
But Riley came back, sitting down on a stool with an
acoustic guitar.

"This is a song for my lovely Nan. It's a song I wrote
especially for her and I've only sung it to her once
before and she promptly fell in love with me. I reckon
if I sing it now, she might just marry me."

Nan leaned closer. "He's going to sing the selkie

song." Her eyes fixed on Riley as he spun the tale of a man in love with a beautiful selkie. The way he sang the ballad, it was as if the two of them were the mortal man and the beautiful creature from the sea.

Jordan watched him, amazed at the depth of emotion he conveyed to the audience…to Nan, tears swimming in her eyes. This was love, she thought to herself. Jordan could see it in Riley's eyes, in the way he smiled at his fiancée.

Riley sang two more songs, both of them sweet love songs, before he nodded to the crowd and stepped off stage, a bottle of beer dangling from his fingers. He was headed directly to Nan, but his trip was interrupted again and again by enthusiastic fans—mostly female.

When he finally reached Nan, he gave her a kiss. "Was it good?"

Her eyes shone. "It was beautiful," she said.

Jordan stood up. "Here, take my seat."

"No, that's all right," Riley said. "How are you, Jordan?"

"I'm great," she said.

Danny came up behind Riley and clapped his brother on the shoulder. "Congratulations, Riley. You got yourself a good one. Now don't do anything to feck it up."

"And you'd do well to take your own advice," Riley teased.

"I could really use some air," Jordan said.

Danny led her to the front door and then out into the cool October night. Jordan wrapped her arm around his as they strolled aimlessly toward the waterfront. The sounds from the pub faded and when they were finally alone, she spoke. "They make a cute couple. It makes me believe that love might be possible."

"You don't believe in love?"

Jordan shook her head. "I think people fall in love, like us. But I'm not sure it can last forever. Sometimes life just gets in the way."

"But then you have someone to help you with life," Danny said. "Two people against the world are a lot better odds than just one."

There were a few people wandering along the quay and they all recognized Danny and said hello. He found a spot for them to sit. Jordan felt a nervous twist in her stomach. She shouldn't have said that to him. It wasn't that she didn't believe in love. She was just used to looking at life in more realistic terms.

"I'm sorry," she said. "Don't listen to me. I don't know what I'm talking about. I never really took the time to think about romance when I was younger. I was too busy trying to keep up. I never dressed up as a bride or secretly planned my wedding or fantasized about what it would be like to find my Prince Charming."

"Love isn't a fairy tale, Jordan. It's life, as real as it gets."

"I know. But I'm supposed to be thrilled by it and it just scares me. It would change everything."

"Yes, it will. It's supposed to."

A moment later, a soft, slow ballad drifted into the cool night air from inside the pub. "There wasn't much room to dance inside. Maybe you'd dance with me here?" Danny asked.

He slipped his arm around her waist then took her

hand in his. His body was strong and hard against hers, their movement generating its own warmth. Jordan tipped her head back and drew a deep breath, then slowly let it go. This was her life, this moment in time, with this man in her arms. Nothing else mattered.

She let her hands trail over his body as she danced, creating a soothing counterpoint to the music. But this wasn't about desire. It was about comfort and protection. Even though the world she'd always known was falling apart, all her dreams disappearing before her eyes, it wasn't completely tragic.

"Maybe we should go back to the party," she said.

"We've made our appearance," Danny said. "I don't think we'll be missed. And I know you'd rather be alone."

"There's plenty of time for that later," she said. "I think maybe I want to learn another one of those Irish dances."

"Yeah?" Danny asked.

Jordan nodded. "Will you teach me?"

"I can do that." He slipped his arms around her waist, then bent closer to kiss her.

When they got back to the pub, Nan rushed up to them both. "We thought you'd left," she said. She held out the presents Danny had set on the end of the bar. "You didn't need to bring us a gift. Didn't you see the invitation?"

"Yes," Jordan said. "But I wanted to. I won't be here for the wedding, so that's what they're for. And you've given me something in return."

"Can I borrow Jordan for a moment?" Nan asked.

"Sure," Danny said. "As long as you give her back. I've grown rather fond of her."

She and Nan walked through the pub and into the kitchen. "This is the only quiet spot in the pub," Nan said. "So tell me, why are you thinking about leaving?"

"Actually, I'm not. I'm thinking of staying. But in case I don't, I wanted to give you the gifts."

"So, are you in love with him? It's all right, you can admit it to me. Believe me, I spent a long time denying it myself. But there's just something about a handsome Irishman that I find completely irresistible."

Jordan sat down on a stool next to the work table, exhaustion overwhelming her. "I've tried to keep everything in perspective," she said. "But I can't seem to help myself. I get lost in the fantasy of living here with him. It's like someone or something has put a spell on me and I'm seeing everything through magic glasses."

"I know exactly how you feel," Nan said. "But don't be so quick to write it off as a fantasy. Maybe you were meant to be here all along."

"Danny told me about your search for your father. You have a place here. I have an Irish last name, that's all."

"You could make a place for yourself," Nan replied. "It's not that hard. And with the Quinns, it seems, the more the merrier."

It wasn't difficult to like Nan. She seemed so sweet and friendly. Jordan had never had many girlfriends. She'd always been so obsessed with her career, she hadn't made time for friendships. And she'd never been interested in hanging out and talking about manicures and boyfriends and designer shoes.

Jordan was amazed at how easy it was to confide in the other woman. Though they came from completely different places, they seemed to have so much in common. She almost felt as if she would have a family here in Ireland if she stayed. "We should probably rejoin the party," Jordan said. "You *are* the guest of honor."

"We should," Nan said. "But promise that we'll see you again, soon. And if you leave, you must say goodbye."

"You should come and see the house. It's almost done. The furniture arrives this next week. Bring Danny's mother and we'll have lunch."

"Then it's decided," Nan said. "Just call when you'd like us to come and we'll be there."

Jordan picked up the presents. "Do you want to open these now or later?"

"Oh, now," Nan said. "I can't stand to wait for a surprise. And I love presents." She paused. "You said before that I'd given you something. What did you mean by that?"

Jordan hesitated, but found no reason to hide her feelings. She could trust Nan. "When I saw you and Riley together, saw how you were that first time we met, how he looked at you and how you looked at him...well, it made me think that I might find that for myself someday. And I don't think I've ever felt that way before."

"Maybe it wasn't just me and Riley," Nan pushed. "Maybe it's Danny?"

"Open it," Jordan said. "I hope you like it."

Nan tore at the paper and pulled open the box then gasped. She reached into the box and withdrew the old silver. "Oh, this is lovely. Look at the monograms. It's hotel silver, isn't it? My favorite restaurant back home uses it. I love it. It's so heavy, so much nicer than what you can buy new."

"Danny didn't understand why I was giving you old silverware." Jordan pointed to the smaller package. "Open that one."

Nan withdrew the book from the paper and smoothed her hand over the cover. Then she opened to the flyleaf. "It's a first printing?"

Jordan nodded. "I know how much you like books. And Yeats is Irish. It seemed like a good gift."

"I—I don't know what to say. It's beautiful." Nan smiled, then reached out and gave Jordan a fierce hug. "Thank you."

Jordan drew a deep breath, satisfied that she'd done well. Someday maybe she'd be planning for her own wedding and her own home. She hoped that she'd have a friend like Nan to talk to when that did happen.

"WHERE ARE WE GOING?" Jordan asked, the bedclothes rumpled around her naked body. "It's Sunday. We're not supposed to get up so early."

"Dress warm," Danny said, tugging on his jeans. "And put on a jacket and some sturdy shoes." He picked up her favorite sweater and laid it on the bed.

"Are we going on a hike?"

Danny bent over and gave her a quick kiss. "A short one."

"Shouldn't we have some breakfast first?"

He sat down next to her and brushed the hair out of her eyes. "After you fell asleep last night, I was just lying here, thinking. I have a theory and I want to check it out."

"A theory about what?"

"Our brownie problem," he said. "I think I might have figured out how they got in."

"No more brownies? I'm all for that." A smile broke across her face as she scrambled out of bed and Danny felt a small measure of relief. Since yesterday evening, Jordan had seemed so melancholy, as if the weight of the world were bearing down on her. He'd tried to coax her worries out of her, and she'd put on a smile and insisted that nothing was wrong. But Danny knew her too well.

He didn't want to think that their time together was coming to an end, or that she'd walk away without a second thought. Hell, how could he compete with a job that she loved and a family who lived on the other side of the Atlantic?

They walked out into the crisp morning air, past the walled garden and the forge and toward the rocky cliffs that separated the green from the ocean. They headed north for a few hundred yards before Danny began to look for the familiar landmark that signaled the entrance to Smuggler's Cove.

"Here," he said, pointing to the narrow pathway between the jagged rocks. "Follow me."

"Where?" Jordan asked.

"Don't worry. I've been down here before. Not for a very long time, but I know the way. Just be careful."

He carefully picked his way along the path, stepping over rocks that had fallen and tossing aside driftwood blocking the way. When he finally reached the end of the path, he jumped down the last three feet, then turned and reached for Jordan.

She stood on the sand and slowly took in her surroundings. "I never knew this was here. It's a little beach. How did you find it?"

"We used to come here when we were kids. We called it Smuggler's Cove. I discovered it. Or at least I thought I had. But if the castle was used for smuggling, then this is where the boats would have come to shore." He turned and scanned the cliff. "If there's a tunnel, it starts right there." He pointed to the cave.

"Can you swim here?" she asked, completely distracted by the prospect of her beachfront castle.

"We used to. The current is pretty strong, but if you stay close to shore, it's fine. Are you ready?"

"For what?"

"We're going to see where the other end of that cave lies. We never had the courage to explore it when we were kids, but if I'm right, it may be the entrance to a tunnel that leads to the house." He pulled a flashlight out of his pocket. "Let's give it a try."

"I'm not going in there," she said. "There might be bats. Or spiders. Or snakes."

"There are no snakes in Ireland."

"Right," Jordan said. "St. Patrick took care of that years ago."

"Maybe this is where the brownies and fairies live." Danny scrambled up the cliff to the entrance of the cave. "If I'm not back in ten minutes, call for help," he said.

Jordan frowned. "Danny, I don't think you should go in there. It could be dangerous. It could collapse and you'd be trapped."

Undeterred, Danny entered the cave. He and his brothers had explored about fifteen feet beyond the entrance before being scared away by strange noises and invisible animals. But as an adult, Danny found nothing in here that was frightening. He knew high tide was hours away and now was the time to see if he was right.

The crates that they'd brought down to sit on years ago were still against the cave wall. And a pile of driftwood that Danny had dragged inside was still where he'd left it so long ago. "Hello!" he shouted.

"Who are you talking to?"

He spun around to find Jordan standing behind him, a worried expression on her face. She squinted against the glare from the flashlight and he motioned her over. "Watch out. This first part is slippery until you get to the sand. The water comes up in here at high tide."

They slowly walked deeper into the cave, the light from the opening fading the further they went. Fifteen feet, twenty, then thirty. And then, to Danny's surprise, the cave suddenly ended. "No," he said.

"This is it?"

He examined the back wall carefully, looking for another way. But there wasn't any. "I guess I was wrong," he said.

They walked back to the entrance and he helped Jordan climb back down to the beach. Danny raked his hands through his hair. So much for his brilliant theories. He plopped down on the beach and stared out at the water. Jordan sat down beside him, smoothing her hand along his shoulders.

"It was a good theory," she said. "And I'm really glad

you showed me the beach. I'm going to see if we can build a stairway down the cliff. It's a perfect spot."

Danny leaned against her and brushed a kiss across her lips. "Stairs are going to take a lot longer than a week to build. Does this mean you're going to stay a few weeks longer?"

"I might be here longer than that," she said. Jordan folded her arms over her knees and fixed her gaze on the horizon. "I think I quit my job."

Danny's breath caught in his throat and he stared at her in disbelief. "You think?"

"Well, I'm not really sure if it's official yet. Of course, I have to finish this project. And my father wants a letter of resignation, which I haven't written. And he could always change his mind, although I don't think he—"

"This is brilliant," Danny said, drawing her into his arms and kissing her. "You won't have to leave."

"Well, I will at some point. I still have an apartment back in New York. Everything I own is there."

"Is this why you were so distant last night? Why you were late for the party?"

Jordan nodded. "I gave him my ultimatum. I told him if he didn't give me the hotel project I'd quit."

"What did he say?" Danny asked.

"He didn't say anything," Jordan replied. "I texted him. I was too nervous to talk to him. It was so much easier. He couldn't bully me and I had control of the conversation. There was no shouting, just little letters on the screen."

Danny took her face in his hands. He couldn't believe it. Everything that he'd been wishing for had suddenly come true. They had time, which meant that he had a chance. "And how do you feel now?"

Jordan frowned. "I'm not sure. There is some relief that I actually managed to express my feelings to my father. There's humiliation that it meant nothing to him. And I guess there's a lot of fear, because I'm not quite sure what I'm going to do to make a living."

"What about Kellan? You said he offered you work."

"It would probably be easier to find a job there. I don't even know if I could legally work here. There are probably all sorts of laws."

He bent closer and gave her another kiss. "But I want you to stay here," he said. "With me. What do you say?"

"I say, I'll think about it."

Danny pulled her down on top of him and settled her hips against his. In a single moment, his life had changed. They had a chance, a way to make this all work out. After Jordan was finished at the castle, she could move in with him. They'd figure out what to do about work and then they'd start a life together.

And somewhere along the way, he'd tell her exactly how he felt. Danny Quinn was in love.

JORDAN STARED AT Danny's profile, outlined by the daylight streaming through the tall windows of the bedroom. She smiled to herself then turned her face into the pillow. A giggle bubbled up and she groaned softly.

This was what it felt like to be in love. It was the most frightening, exhilarating, confusing feeling she'd ever had in her life. All the silly stereotypes were true. She felt as if her head was in the clouds, as if she was walking on air, as if nothing would ever be the same again.

Why hadn't it snuck up slowly? Why had it hit her now, while he was asleep beside her and she wasn't expecting it? Jordan's impulse was to question her own feelings, but even that didn't work. She was in love with Danny Quinn, no doubts, no hesitation.

She pushed up from the pillow and took another look. That face, those dark lashes and those beautiful lips. She'd grown so familiar with his features that she almost took them for granted.

She'd decided to stay in Ireland for a little while. Her savings could stand a year or two without work, if she was frugal. But, in truth, she wanted to see where all of this was leading.

Jordan leaned over and dropped a soft kiss on his mouth, then waited to see if he was ready to wake up. When he didn't, she kissed him again, this time running her tongue over the part in his lips.

Danny moaned softly, then opened his eyes. "What are you doing?"

"Kissing you," she whispered.

"While I'm sleeping? Don't we do enough of that while we're awake?" He rolled over on his stomach and stared at her, his cheek pressed into the pillow. "If you expect sex while I'm sleeping, then we're going to have a serious problem. I need to have some time for rest."

"That's not what I want," she said. "I need to talk to you."

"About what?"

"About the subject we've been so cautiously avoiding."

"The crazy way your hair looks in the morning?" he asked.

Jordan grabbed her pillow and hit him squarely in the face. "No." She paused. "Is it really that bad?" She crawled off the bed and ran to the bathroom. "You could have told me this sooner," she shouted, grabbing a brush.

"I'm just taking a piss," Danny replied.

"In the bed?"

"No. I'm teasing you. Making a joke. Your hair looks grand."

Jordan quickly brushed through the tangled strands, then ran back into the bedroom and hopped beneath the covers. "There. That's better."

"I love the way you look in the morning," Danny growled. He grabbed her and pulled her on top of him. He was hard and ready, his erection pressed against her belly. "So what can I do for you this morning, my fairy queen?"

Jordan stared down into his handsome face, then smoothed her fingers over his brow. She'd grown so used to this, their time together in the early morning, the quiet conversations and the lazy seductions. How would she ever live without him? "I thought we ought to talk about what's going to happen once the house is finished. We've only got a few days left. They're going to bring the furniture day after tomorrow and you'll be finished the day after that."

"Actually, I'm already finished," Danny said. "I've just been making work the past few days. I made some tools for the fireplaces. And I was thinking about doing andirons for the fireplace in the breakfast room. Even though that room had just a grate."

"No, if you're finished, then that's it."

"I don't want to be finished. I like it here. I like this bed. And I like waking up with you in the morning."

"I don't have a job after this project is done."

"You need to talk to Kellan and tell him that you're interested in his offer."

"I will," Jordan said. "I just have a lot of things to think about right now. And I've decided that I'm going to take some time before I make any big decisions. I'm going to look for a place to stay here and—"

"You'll stay with me," Danny said.

"But I should—"

"You'll stay with me," he insisted, his tone firm.

Jordan smiled and gave him a hug. "I was hoping you'd say that. I'm going to have to go back to New York at some point to sublet my apartment and move some stuff out, but that can probably wait."

"I think we should do some traveling. We could go to Paris or London or Rome. Some lady paid me a boat-load of money for my last job and I think we should spend it."

Jordan ran her hand over the rough stubble of his beard. "Paris would be fun," she said. "But we'd go Dutch. I'd have to pay my own way or I refuse to travel with you."

Danny's hands spanned her waist and he pulled her beneath him. "Do you think they have soft beds like this in Paris?"

"I'm sure they do."

Jordan closed her eyes as he kissed her, enjoying the flood of desire that snaked through her body. His palm skimmed over her naked breast and his mouth teased at the places that only he knew.

"We won't have many days left in this bed," she murmured, furrowing her fingers through his hair. "I suppose we ought to make the best of it."

"You remember, I do have a bed at my cottage. We won't be sleeping on the floor."

"I know," Jordan said. "But this was our first bed. It's special."

"We could always take it with us," Danny suggested.

"If you have an extra ten thousand pounds, I'll sell it to you," she said.

"Bloody hell. You paid that much for this bed?"

"It's a very special bed. And it's going into the master suite when the movers come."

"When are they coming?"

"Day after tomorrow. We stage the whole house that day. Top to bottom. I've hired some women from the village to help and I have seven movers coming. They're bringing everything from the warehouse. And at the end of the day, the house will be done. We'll have to be out the next morning."

"I'm going to start moving my tools back tomorrow," he said. "I should be cleared out of the laundry in a few days."

Jordan nodded. "I wish my father could see this place," she said. "I've sent him photos, but it's not the same. It's so much more impressive when you see it in person."

"Feck him," Danny said. "He doesn't appreciate you the way I do. He doesn't deserve you."

"Yes," Jordan said. "Feck him. I don't need him anymore."

"No, you don't. You're clever and talented and you can do this for yourself."

Jordan slipped her arms around his neck. "I'm glad you believe in me."

"It's not a difficult thing to do, Jordan."

They made love quietly and slowly, enjoying a long lazy morning in bed. And, through it all, there was no more fear or hesitation. She didn't have to think about leaving him. They had many more mornings ahead of them.

And on one of those mornings, she might tell him what was in her heart, how she'd fallen in love even though she'd tried so hard not to. How he'd captured her heart the very first time she'd set eyes on him.

But that could wait. She had all the time in the world.

8

THE MANOR HOUSE was dark and silent. Danny lay in bed, Jordan asleep beside him. He turned to look at her and smiled to himself. They'd come home from a leisurely dinner in the village and immediately crawled into bed. But this time, they hadn't made love. Instead, they'd spoken softly about their plans for the future.

He drew a deep breath. For now, she was going to stay. She'd furnish the house, then pack her things and move in with him. It wasn't meant to be permanent, but it was a step in the right direction.

Danny closed his eyes, unable to relax. He couldn't sleep. His mind was filled with possibilities now that Jordan was going to be a part of his life for a bit longer. It was all he'd really wanted, just a little more time.

He swung his legs off the bed, dressed only in his boxers. The air was chilly and he rubbed his arms as he walked out of the bedroom. Finny and Mogue looked up at him as he passed, but he held out his hand to stop them from rising.

He knew the house well enough that he needed no more light that the moonlight that poured through the mullioned windows. His feet were quiet against the stone stairs and he ducked into the library, heading for the small table that held a whiskey decanter.

He crossed the room and poured himself a whiskey then headed for the kitchen. Since the Shakespeare had gone missing, they hadn't found any other trace of intruders.

Danny suspected one of the workmen had come inside looking for help and left the footprint. As for the book, perhaps it had fallen out of the crate on the way to the house. Still, there were moments when he felt as if he were being watched. Ghosts. The house was probably filled with all sorts of spirits, both good and evil.

As he stepped inside the door to the kitchen, Danny froze. A figure stood at the refrigerator, the light from the interior creating an eerie silhouette. He knew immediately that it wasn't Jordan. She was sound asleep upstairs. "What the hell—"

The man spun around, a half-eaten sandwich in his hand. Danny recognized the face immediately. "Bartie?" The elderly man made a break for the butler's pantry door, but Danny was quicker. He caught him by the arm and dragged him to a stop. To his surprise, Bartie didn't offer any resistance. "What the hell are you doing in here?"

"Having myself a sandwich. I was doing a—a spot of night work in the garden and felt a twinge in my stomach."

"How did you get in?"

"The door. It was—unlocked."

"No, it wasn't. I checked all the doors and the windows. Everything is locked up tight."

"I have a right to be here," Bartie said.

"You have a right to trespass?"

"This is *my* house. *Mine.* You're the ones who are trespassing."

Either Bartie was delusional or drunk. Danny was determined to find out which it was and then find out exactly how he got inside. "Come on," he muttered. He dragged him along with him to the library. When they got inside, Danny flipped on a lamp, then pointed to a chair next to the fireplace. "Sit."

"I'm the host here. You're the guest. Don't tell me what to do."

The sandwich still clutched in his hand, Bartie watched Danny with suspicious eyes. "I could stand a whiskey," he said.

Danny strolled over to the small bar table and poured a measure into a tumbler. Perhaps it would loosen Bartie's tongue.

"Don't be stingy there, boy. A little more would be appreciated."

Stubborn old sot, Danny thought as he handed him the whiskey. "How many times have you been in the house, Bartie? I mean, before I caught you."

"I come and go as I please," he said. "It's my house."

"How is that possible?"

"I'm the heir to Castle Cnoc."

"You?"

The old man took a sip of the whiskey then returned to eating his sandwich. "My grandfather owned the place. He inherited it from his father."

"You're a Carrick?"

Bartie nodded, then wiped his hand on his pants and held it out to Danny. "Bartholomew G. Carrick the third. Pleasure to meet you."

Danny took Bartie's hand and shook it. This was growing more bizarre with every moment that passed. The man who'd been digging holes for months in the garden was the former heir to Castle Cnoc. "You've been sneaking into the house?"

He nodded.

"How? I've made sure the place has been locked up tighter than a drum. And there are the dogs."

"I have my ways," Bartie said. "Secret ways. I'm not about to tell you." He paused. "And your dogs don't bark at someone who's been feeding them bits of beef every day."

"You will tell me how you got in or I'll call the gardai. And they'll haul you off to jail. If you're honest about all this, I may let you go without reporting you to either the authorities or Jordan."

"She doesn't belong here. I do."

"Bartie, I'm not sure how it happened, but I know that this house doesn't belong to you. Not anymore."

The older man blinked at him, as if he didn't fully comprehend the complexities of property ownership. "It's been in my family for generations."

"And now it isn't. Besides, why would you want this great hulk of a place? It's impossible to keep up. It would take thousands, hell, millions, to keep it looking like this. Myself, I've always preferred a tidy little cottage."

"I have a cottage," Bartie said. "In the village. It's lovely."

"I have a place of my own in Ballykirk. Men like us don't need all these trappings. This place is like a museum. We're just regular blokes."

Bartie nodded, then drained the rest of his whiskey. He held out the glass. "Another," he ordered.

Danny decided to keep him drinking and talking. "So, you've been coming in and wandering around at night because you can't bear to part with the family estate? But what's with the holes in the garden?"

Bartie leaned forward. "I'm trying to find the treasure."

"What treasure?"

"The gold and silver my grandfather buried in the garden. Before he lost his fortune, he hid a chest somewhere on the estate, to save it from his creditors. He planned to come back for it, but he died suddenly and the family fell into financial ruin. That's when they had to sell Castle Cnoc."

Danny wasn't sure of the legalities of the situation. Would buried money belong to the current landowner or the heir of the person that buried it? Either way, Bartie would probably have some legal claim. "And have you found anything?"

He shook his head. "Not yet. But I will. I've been looking now for seventeen years. It's got to be here somewhere."

"And you've looked in the house?"

"Oh, yes, I know every inch of this house and it's not here. Once she leaves I'll have much more freedom to look. The new owners won't be around much, I reckon."

He gave Danny a shrewd look. "If you help me and we find it, I'll give you twenty percent."

"If you show me how you got in," Danny murmured, "I might consider it."

"It's a secret," Bartie said, grinning. He tapped his nose. "Only I know. A family secret passed down to the heir to Castle Cnoc."

"Of course if you're talking about the smuggler's tunnel, we already know about that."

Danny's question had the desired effect. Though there had always been talk of a tunnel out to the coast, Bartie would be the one to know. The old man's face flushed red and he seemed to grow more agitated. "Perhaps it's time to call the authorities?"

"I haven't done anything wrong. This house belongs to me."

"Bartie, you know that's not true. And besides trespassing, they might want to add some other charges as well. Stalking, harassment, theft. You could be facing ten, maybe twenty years. And what about Daisy? She could be charged as your accomplice."

"I—I—but—Daisy was only helping me search the grounds. She knew nothing about me coming into the house. And *theft*—I only took a copy of *A Midsummer Night's Dream* so Miss Kennally would think maybe there were fairies."

Danny scowled. "What about the vase? And the ring?"

"I broke the vase accidentally. And I thought the ring might be a clue. I put it back." Bartie looked offended.

"Show me the tunnel right now and I'll make sure none of this ever gets back to the authorities."

"Yes." Bartie paused. "Maybe that would be best."

"Danny?"

They both turned to find Jordan standing in the doorway, dressed in only a faded T-shirt. Her eyes went wide when she caught sight of Bartie and she pulled the bottom of the shirt down to cover her backside.

"What are you doing here, Bartie? It's late."

"Bartie is our resident brownie," Danny said. "He's been in and out of this house—what?—a hundred times since he started working for you."

"More before that," Bartie said. "It's not hard." He walked over to the center bookshelf on the far wall. "It's this center shelf. You just give it a quick shove, like this and—" He pushed and the bookcase suddenly became a door. "Simple, really. The stairway leads to a tunnel and the tunnel comes out on the cliffs."

"Why did you come in?"

"Bartie's been looking for treasure."

"First, I thought it was in the house, but I've been over this place with a magnifying glass before you showed up. Swimming pool too. Thought it might be there, but it wasn't. The garden was the next logical spot." He frowned. "It's here somewhere. I know it."

"What were you doing in my room that night?"

"Hoping to steal a key," he said. "Crawling through that tunnel's been hard on the back," he complained. "Would rather come through the front door, I would."

The three of them stood silently for a long time. "What do you want to do with him?" Danny asked.

Jordan sighed. "Just finish the garden, Bartie. I want to see roses in there before the end of the week. Stop digging holes, stop sneaking into the house. If there was

hidden treasure here, you would have found it already."
She looked over at Danny. "I'm going to bed. Are you
coming?"

"You don't want to see where this passageway goes?"
he asked, surprised.

"No! It's the middle of the night. We'll look at it tomorrow." She stumbled out of the room, grumbling, "I
can't believe Bartie was the brownie. All of that worry
for nothing."

THE NEXT FEW DAYS at Castle Cnoc were a flurry of activity. The moment Jordan got a look at the smuggler's
tunnel, she insisted that it had to be renovated before
the owner arrived: electric lighting installed, the walls
freshly painted and the tile floor restored. She would
even have the blueprints for the house redrawn to show
the new discovery.

Danny had been left to find work for himself, staying
out from underfoot as much as he could. The furniture
was being delivered that morning and though he'd offered to help, Jordan had suggested that he help Bartie
finish up the plantings in the garden.

In truth, Danny was glad to be banished from the
house. Since the movers had arrived at eight that morning, Jordan had been edgy and curt, overwhelmed with
the details of examining each piece before it was placed
in the proper room. Jordan had also hired five women
from the village to give the manor house a final polish.
They were to wash the new linens, make the beds,
unpack china and silver in the butler's pantry and carefully arrange all the bits and pieces of decor that she
had chosen over the past seventeen months. When she

wasn't dragging furniture from one spot to the other, Jordan was directing traffic and barking out orders.

Danny wandered back outside and headed to the walled garden. After the confrontation with Bartie two nights before, the old man had focused all his energy on finishing the planting. Danny felt a bit sorry for him. After years of searching for his treasure, he'd finally decided to give up looking.

Bartie had brought a crew from the village to help yesterday and they'd worked all day to get nearly a hundred rose bushes planted. Now he was spreading mulch between the plants and the crushed-stone paths.

Danny grabbed a shovel that was leaning against the wall and stepped inside the garden, ready to give the old man a hand. But as he shoved the spade into the mulch, an image flashed in his mind. There was one place that Bartie might not have searched.

"Bartie," he called, motioning the man over. "Grab your shovel and come with me."

"I have to finish. Miss Jordan wants this done by the end of the day."

"We can take a break. I'll cover for you with Jordan."

Bartie joined him and Danny headed toward the cliff. "Have you ever been down to the cove?"

"When I was a kid. Gettin' down the cliff is tricky at my age."

"And you know about the cave?" Danny asked.

Bartie shook his head. "I don't know of any cave."

"Well, I'm sure your great-grandfather knew about it. I suspect they used it to store smuggled goods until they could move them through the tunnel. I'm thinking that maybe your great-grandfather buried his treasure in that cave."

"It makes sense," Bartie said. "What if we find it?"

"We'll cross that bridge when we come to it," Danny said.

He helped Bartie navigate the narrow path down the cliffs, then showed him how to get inside the cave. The flashlight he'd used for the last trip to the cave was still in his pocket and he turned it on. "He'd have to bury anything past the reach of the water," Danny said. "You can see on the wall how far up it comes."

They started at the back wall of the cave, working in the wavering light. Almost immediately, they struck something metallic buried in the sand. Bartie looked up at him, wide-eyed, then bent down and began to brush the sand away with his hands.

Slowly, he uncovered a small metal box, the kind that usually held ammunition. Danny held his breath, hoping that Bartie wasn't about to be disappointed. "Can you get it open?" he asked.

"You do it," Bartie said. "I'm not sure I care to look."

"Let's get it into the light," Danny said.

They hurried back to the cave entrance and set the box down on the ground. It was barely rusted, the dark-green paint still visible. The box wasn't locked. Danny grabbed the top and pulled it back.

"Jaysus, Mary and Joseph," Bartie whispered. "It's the treasure. It's gold."

The old man was right. The box was filled with gold coins, hundreds of them. Danny picked one up and examined it. "It's a British sovereign," he said. "Looks like a coin from the Victorian age."

"But my great-grandfather buried the treasure in the 1920s," Bartie said.

"This might not be his treasure. This might be gold from the smugglers."

"How much do you reckon it's worth?" Bartie asked.

"I don't know," Danny said. "A lot. It's gold." He took a deep breath. "We're going to have to show this to Jordan. It was found on private property. I don't know what the law says."

They made their way back up the cliff and Danny ordered Bartie to take the box of gold to the garden and wait there. With every step he took toward the house, he thought about keeping the gold a secret from Jordan, of letting Bartie walk away with his treasure—even though it wasn't the treasure he was looking for.

Though he knew Jordan well, Danny had no idea how she'd react to this interesting development. Would she insist that her clients get the gold? Or would she find a way to compromise? The new owner was certainly rich enough. A movie star like Maggie Whitney made millions for each picture.

He found Jordan standing in the foyer, a clipboard clutched in her arms. He strode up to her and gently grabbed her elbow. "Jordan," he murmured. "I need to see you out in the garden."

"Not now," she said. "They're just bringing in the dining room table and I need to make sure they put it together properly."

"This is an emergency," Danny said.

She looked up from her clipboard. "Can't it wait?"

"No, it can't." He took her hand and pulled her out the terrace door and down the path to the walled garden.

"What is it? Is Bartie all right?"

"Bartie is fine," Danny said. "We found the treasure."

Jordan stopped short. "*What?* Where?"

"In the cave," he said. "A big box of gold coins." He squeezed her hand. "What are you going to do?"

She drew a deep breath. "What do you think I should do?"

"I think you should let Bartie keep his treasure," Danny replied. "But I'm not the boss, you are."

He watched as she thought through her options. Then she glanced up at him. "Why am I out here? There can't be anything more important than moving the furniture into the house. You and Bartie get back to work on the rose garden."

With that, Jordan turned on her heel and strode back inside, leaving Danny to wonder at what had just happened. She'd completely ignored everything he'd just told her—

He grinned, then walked back to the garden. There was a reason he loved Jordan and he had no doubt that his feelings weren't going to change.

Odd how the prospect of falling in love had once scared the hell out of him. Now, it made him feel as though he was sitting on top of the world. Danny didn't care that it had happened so fast, or that they hadn't completely decided on a future together. Jordan wasn't going home tomorrow, she was coming to live with him. Tomorrow, they'd start their life together.

Bartie was waiting for him, the box at his feet. "I guess you can just take that old metal box and everything inside it home, Bartie, and I'll finish up in the garden. Jordan isn't interested in anything you've found." Danny pressed his finger to his lips. "But I wouldn't go passing this story around the village or she might change her mind. Keep your good fortune to yourself."

"I'll do that," Bartie said, reaching down and picking up the box. "Yes, I will. I'll do that." He pulled a coin out of the box and handed it to Danny. "Here. It will bring you luck."

Danny watched as Bartie hurried off, the box tucked under his arm. He chuckled softly. Things had a way of working out just grand.

JORDAN STOOD IN THE DOORWAY. Her hair, twisted into a tidy knot earlier, now tumbled around her flushed face. Her clothes were dirty and wrinkled and she felt exhaustion overwhelming her.

"Almost done?"

She turned to look at Danny and smiled. "Almost. We're just missing a sofa. Either it never got delivered to the warehouse or they misplaced it there. But that's it. Everything else arrived in one piece, no scratches, no breakage."

Danny reached out and gathered her in his arms. "Congratulations. You did it."

"I did. Almost. I have to finish my paperwork tonight and email that to the office and then make a quick double check of my list and I'll be done."

"We should celebrate," he said. "I'll take you out tonight and we'll have some fun." He pulled the gold coin out of his pocket. "I've come into a little bit of money."

She laughed. "Don't show me that. I might ask where it came from."

"You did a good thing," he whispered, his breath warm on her hair.

"Right now, all I really need is a nice long foot massage, a hot bath and a warm bed."

Danny grinned. "I can do that," he said. "In fact, I'm good at all those things."

Jordan kissed his cheek. "We're back to the caretaker's cottage for now. I'll be out in a minute. I want to call your mom and Nan and see if they'd like to come tomorrow morning for a tour. And I have to track down that—" Her cell rang and she pulled it out of her pocket. "This might be my missing sofa."

"I'll see you in a few minutes," Danny said. He wandered through the doors to the terrace and Jordan smiled as she watched him move. She'd worried for so long over the day they'd have to part, but now, all those worries had disappeared.

Her phone rang again and Jordan looked at the caller I.D. then winced. It was her father. She hadn't spoken to him since their exchange of text messages earlier that week. She was in no mood to talk to him now. She groaned, still staring at the phone. "I don't have time for this right now."

She walked over to an upholstered bench and sat down, then answered the call. "Hello, Daddy. How are you?"

"It's not your father, Jordan, it's your mother. I want you to talk to your father and give him a chance to apologize to you. Don't argue with him, just listen."

"I don't want to talk to him, Mom," she said. "He made his decision and now I've made mine. And I'm all right with that. It's for the best. It's time for me to move on with my life."

"It certainly is not!" her mother declared. "Here he is."

"No, I don't want to— Hi, Daddy." Her heart began to pound in her chest and she took in a deep breath.

"Your mother wanted me to call. I'm sorry I was so unreasonable with you. And I've taken Matt off the hotel project and assigned it to you. You need to finish up this week and get back to New York."

"Daddy, I'm not sure I—"

"I'm not going to beg you, Jordan. Just get back here and we'll smooth things out. You'll have your project and now you're going to have to prove my trust in you is worth it."

Jordan slowly shook her head. "I'll be back in New York in a few days. I'll talk to you then."

Jordan turned off the phone and slowly walked outside. She found Danny in the cottage, sitting on the edge of the bed. His smile faded as his gaze met hers. "What's wrong? Is your sofa lost, then?"

"My father just called," Jordan said.

"Did he apologize?" Danny asked.

She shook her head. "He just offered me the hotel job. I guess after my mother heard that I quit, she was very upset. She was afraid I wasn't going to come home so she told my father he had to give me the project."

"Do you still want the project?" Danny asked.

"I—I don't know."

The expression on his face told her the whole story. This was what she'd wanted all along and now that it had been offered, Danny wasn't at all confident that she would turn it down.

"Hey, this is good, right?" Danny said, forcing a smile. "This is what you've been working for."

"I really wanted to earn it," she said. "I didn't want it handed to me like some bribe."

"You did earn it."

"No. I'm sure my mother threatened to divorce my father and take half his money. She does that when she doesn't get her own way. Only this time she probably meant it."

Danny grabbed her hand and pulled her down next to him. "You don't have to make a decision right now. Think about it. You can take some time."

"We're going to be done here in a few days. The new owners will be here for Christmas. I've hired a house-keeper and a caretaker. After tomorrow, I'm finished. He wants me to start the new project next week."

"Next week?"

She nodded.

"How long? To finish the project?"

"A year at least," Jordan said. "It wouldn't be like this project. I'd have a huge crew, lots of resources. It would be my first really major project for Kencor."

"This wasn't a major project?"

Jordan shook her head. "This is a private home. He called it my little decorating job. I could have done this in my sleep. Since I met you, I have kind of been doing it in my sleep."

"This is bollocks," Danny muttered. "How the hell am I supposed to compete with a feckin' hotel in Manhattan?"

"I don't want to go," Jordan said. "You're right. It is my choice. And if I choose to stay with you, my father will have to live with that."

Danny pulled her into a hug, raining kisses over her face. "Tell me you really mean that," he murmured. "Just tell me so I can put aside this sick feeling in my gut. I don't want to lose you, Jordan. I'm not ready to let you go."

Jordan didn't speak, but stood up beside the bed and began to take her clothes off. When she was completely undressed, she helped Danny out of his clothes then pulled him down on the bed. She didn't want to think about all of her choices right now. She wanted to lose herself in the feel of his body against hers, in the taste of his mouth.

Making love to him was the only thing that made sense right now. He made her happy, happier than she'd ever been in her life. Home was no longer in New York. Home was wrapped in Danny's arms.

9

DANNY WOKE UP LONG BEFORE DAWN, listening to the sounds of Ballykirk as the village slowly came to life. At first, it was just the fishing boats heading out of the harbor and then a lorry or two passing by.

Tossing the covers aside and swinging his feet off the bed, he stood and stretched. As soon as the dogs heard him, they scampered into the bedroom, anxious for their breakfast. "Hi, boys," he whispered, giving them each a pet.

Jordan's plane was due to leave at ten. Danny had insisted on taking her to the airport, but she'd decided to drive herself and leave her car in the car park. She'd promised she'd be back in a few days, after she'd settled everything with her parents.

In truth, Danny still wasn't sure he wanted her to leave. Even though he believed she was going to settle her affairs and come right back to him, there was a niggling doubt that her father might talk her into staying.

He couldn't imagine a future with Jordan in New York and him in Ireland. Though the two places were only a six-hour plane ride apart, there was still an ocean between them. They'd be living completely different lives. But it wasn't just their lives, it was their ideas of what constituted happiness. For Jordan, it was professional success and for him, it had become all about love in the past month.

Here in Ireland, she could be in control of her own destiny. With Kellan's help, she could build a business to be proud of. There were possibilities in the U.K., in Europe. So many interesting things to do.

But Jordan had spent her life trying to please her father and to prove her worth in her family. It was a strangely dysfunctional relationship, but one that she couldn't seem to resist.

Danny wandered out to the fireplace and threw some peat on the fire, anxious to take the chill out of the air. Her bag was open on the sofa near the fireplace, packed with a change of clothes. He sat down and picked through it, pulling out a T-shirt and inhaling the scent.

Was this all he'd be left with, Danny wondered. Just faint memories of a woman he'd once loved and then lost. He tucked the T-shirt under his arm. She wasn't going to stay long, he told himself. There was nothing to worry over.

Danny walked back to the bedroom and sat on the edge of the bed. He pressed a gentle kiss to Jordan's forehead, then drew a deep breath, committing the scent of her hair to memory. They'd spent nearly every minute together since his first day at Castle Cnoc and now, they'd be apart.

His time with Jordan had brought him a love deeper than anything he'd ever expected. Danny felt as if they had already spent a lifetime together. He'd never known a woman so intimately nor had he allowed any woman to know him in that way. Jordan had become a part of him, the part that made him feel alive and aware.

He pulled back the covers and crawled back into bed, snuggling up to her naked body. She stirred then opened her eyes. "It can't be morning already," she murmured.

"It is," Danny replied. "Although it's only been about four hours since you fell asleep."

Jordan groaned, then stretched her arms above her head. "How am I going to do without you in my bed? I'll have to just get reacquainted with my vibrator."

"You have one of those?" Danny chuckled. "Make sure you bring that back with you."

He kissed the curve of her neck. Her skin was so soft and he could feel her pulse beating beneath his lips. God, it was strange something as insignificant as a kiss would seem so important to him. Everything was important—the sound of her voice, the feel of her hand in his, the way she said his name...

The first light of dawn illuminated the room and Jordan glanced again at the clock. "I have to get up." She raked her hands through her tousled hair as she sat up beside him.

Danny watched as she silently got dressed. When she was finished, she sat on the edge of the bed and smoothed her fingers over his temple, brushing aside a strand of hair. Danny looked up at her. "You could still change your mind," he murmured. "You could take off all your clothes and crawl into bed with me and go to New York some other day."

"I don't want to leave," Jordan said. "But I have to.

I won't be gone long, I promise. I'll be back before you know it."

"What if you decide to stay?" He raised up, bracing his arm beside him and leaning closer to her. This was no time to keep his feelings to himself. He was going to say it all right now, just so she knew exactly how much he needed her. "You have everything waiting for you back there. All you have here is me."

"And that's everything," she said. "To me."

"Me, too," he said softly.

Her eyes flooded with tears and Danny groaned, pulling her into a hug. He wanted to say the words. They'd been on his lips for days now, yet he was scared that Jordan wasn't ready to return the sentiment. He loved her, but did she love him?

Danny reached out and cupped her cheek in his palm. "Promise that you'll come back to me," he whispered. "Promise you won't let your family talk you into staying."

She drew a ragged breath. "I promise."

"I'll miss you, Jordan. I don't think you realize how much."

Jordan smiled, then bent close and dropped a kiss on his lips. "I'll miss you, too, Danny."

He fell back onto the pillow and laughed, throwing his arm over his head. "I sure hope to hell you aren't *leanan sidhe* or I'm going to drop dead the moment you walk out the door."

She grabbed his face and kissed him again, a kiss filled with longing and sorrow and silent promises. "I'm not a fairy. And you're not going to die when I leave you. I—I have to go."

"Let me get dressed and I'll—"

"No, I want to leave you right here, in this cottage, all curled up in bed with Finny and Mogue asleep in front of the door. This is how I want to remember you, all rumpled from sleep and naked beneath the sheets. And when I come back, I want you to be here just like this."

"I'm actually contemplating staying in bed until you come back. I'm not sure I'll be able to do anything else, I'll be so consumed with loneliness and despair." He tried for a lighthearted tone.

"Get up and get some work done." She gave him another quick kiss and then walked to the door. Jordan picked up her bag and gave him one last look. "I'll talk to you soon," she murmured.

"Call me when you get in?"

She nodded. "I'll do that." She crossed the room and kissed him again. "Let's just say goodbye like it's any other day," she murmured. "I'll be back soon. I promise."

As she walked out of the bedroom, Danny wondered what it would be like the next time they saw each other. Would the attraction still be so intense or would it have cooled? Would they pick up where they'd left off or would they need to get to know each other again? These were all questions that worried him. Danny knew they'd have to figure out a way to get through the confusion and back to where they belonged.

He jumped out of bed and hurried to the front door, standing naked in the damp morning air. She saw him and waved from inside the car, then turned on the ignition. "Come back," he murmured to himself.

If she came back, this would become home. His family would become her family. They said absence made the heart grow fonder. Danny was counting on that to get him through the next few days.

He drew a deep breath of the morning air and then cursed loudly.

"Oh, to hell with this."

JORDAN STOOD AT the elevator and watched as the lighted numbers above the door moved downward. She'd been back in Manhattan for exactly one day, just enough time to sleep, sort through her mail and do laundry before grabbing a cab to the office.

The flight back had been uneventful, except for one thing. Whether it was the regret at leaving Ireland or the doubts she had about leaving Danny, she'd decided that it was time for her to have a serious talk with her father.

The elevator opened in front of her and she stepped inside, smoothing her hands over the designer suit she wore. She'd assumed that once she was back in her own bed, wearing her regular wardrobe she'd start to feel more like herself. But New York seemed like a foreign country now and she felt oddly out of place in the midst of all the noise and chaos.

When she stepped out of the elevator on the seventeenth floor, a familiar face greeted her. "Miss Kennally! Welcome back. You look...fabulous."

Jordan frowned at Isabelle, their receptionist. "Fabulous?"

"There's something different about you. You look... sunny."

"Well, I feel sunny," Jordan said with a smile. "Is my father in? I need to talk to him right away."

"He's in. You'll have to check with Anne Marie to see if he's available."

"Great," Jordan said. "Well, wish me luck."

"Luck," Isabelle replied. "Miss Kennally?"

Jordan turned back to her. "Yes?"

"I do hope you plan to stay. Rumor around the office was that you quit. That's not true, is it?"

Jordan smiled. "I think it is."

When she reached her office, just three doors down from her father's, Jordan dropped off her coat and briefcase. The sooner she got this over with the better. It wouldn't do to delay and lose her nerve.

Jordan glanced down at her hands, her fingers twisted together so tightly that they were losing circulation. Conversations with her father had always been very cold and businesslike. But today, she hoped to appeal to his emotions. She wanted, no, she needed his blessing.

In truth, she expected it would be much worse. He'd throw her out on her ear, maybe even refuse to pay her for the Castle Cnoc project. He'd disown her, forbid her to come to family functions. Andrew Kennally hadn't gotten to where he was today by being a nice guy.

Drawing a deep breath, she headed toward his office. His assistant was sitting at her desk and Jordan pointed at the door. "He's in?"

"Yes. But I think he's on the phone. Can I make an appointment for you?"

"No," Jordan said. "I need to talk to him right now."

"But, Miss Kennally, I don't think he wants to be disturbed."

"I'm his daughter. I'm allowed to disturb him." Before the assistant could stop her, Jordan opened the door and stepped inside. Her father was sitting at his desk, his back to her, his feet kicked up on the credenza. She listened to his conversation and it was obvious he was discussing the closing on the hotel project.

Jordan sat and waited patiently, silently going over all she planned to say. She was putting her future on the line, but it had to be done.

The entire way home, she'd thought about what she was giving up by moving to Ireland. She loved her family, but she loved Danny more. He was the one who believed in her, who supported all her dreams. Her future was with him.

Her father hung up the phone, then slowly turned around to face her. Andrew Kennally was a handsome man of nearly sixty. His graying hair was set off by a deeply tanned face. He wore custom-made suits and hand-stitched shirts and Italian shoes that cost more than the rent on a one-bedroom apartment on the Upper East Side. And all of that made him very intimidating.

"Hello, Daddy."

"You're back," he said, nodding at her. "It seems like you just left."

"I've been gone for almost eighteen months," Jordan reminded him.

"Right," he said. "Well, welcome back. I'm sure you want to jump right back into work so…run along."

"That's what I want to talk to you about," Jordan

said. "If you'll remember, we had a discussion on the phone not too long ago about the hotel project."

"Yes. I remember. It's still yours, if you want it."

"Why?" she asked. "I know you didn't want to give it to me. Why did you change your mind?"

"Your mother can be very persuasive."

"So, it's not because you trust my work. In fact, you don't think I deserve it, do you?"

"That's neither here nor there," he said. "You have the damn project. We close day after tomorrow so I'd suggest you sit down with your brother, Matt, and get up to speed. He's been doing all the preliminary work."

"I don't think that's going to be necessary," Jordan said.

"What? You think you're just going to hit the ground running?"

"No. I'm not going to hit the ground at all. I don't want the job, Daddy. I'm going to go back to Ireland. I'm quitting Kencor."

"Quit? Don't be ridiculous. You'll never find another job like this."

"I hope not. This hasn't been all that great. And you've been a horrible boss. You've always favored my brothers more than me and I'm tired of that. I proved myself capable of handling larger projects, but that didn't make a difference to you."

He shook his head. "Your mother isn't going to stand for this," he warned.

"I don't care. It's time for me to make my own way in the world. I've met a man. I'm in love and I'm happy."

"This is about a man? You're quitting your job for a man?"

"No," Jordan said. "I'm quitting my job because I need to find a place where my talents are appreciated."

"Oh, we're not going to get into all that warm fuzzy stuff. We don't do that here. I don't run around telling my employees how wonderful they are. That's not the way I run things."

"Maybe you should. People might not think you're such a jerk."

"You don't have any loyalty to me?"

"You're my father and I will always love you. But as a boss, you kind of suck. I've worked my ass off here and I deserved more than you gave me. But that's all water under the bridge. I just want you to give me your blessing and then I'll get out of your hair."

"What is this really about?" he asked. "What happened to you in Ireland?"

"Perspective," she said. "I got some perspective. I realized that there's a lot more to life than work. And I don't want to miss out on the good stuff."

"I don't like ultimatums," her father muttered, wagging his finger at her.

"I'm not giving you an ultimatum. I've made my decision, Daddy." She stood up. "I'm going back to Ireland in a few days. I'd like to come out and see you and Mom this weekend. I expect I'm going to have to explain everything to her."

"She's going to kill me, you know. She'll blame me for letting you go."

"I'll tell her that it wasn't you." She walked around his desk and threw her arms around his neck, kissing him on the cheek. "Thanks for everything. For the job.

For the opportunity. I really am grateful." She slowly straightened to find him smiling at her. "What?"

"You used to hug me like that when you were little. I liked it. I still do."

Jordan smiled, then walked to the door. She gave her father a wave, then strode down the hall toward her office. Right now, she wanted to find a quiet place to call Danny. And after she was done talking to him, she'd clean out her office, pack up her apartment and figure out how to get her things to Ireland.

She found Marcy, her assistant, flipping through a sheaf of papers on her desk. "You're back," Marcy said. She stared at her for a long moment. "You look different. Have you lost weight?"

"Actually, I've gained ten pounds," Jordan said. "I think it looks good on me, what do you think?"

"I think you look…happy."

"I am," she said. "I just quit my job. Don't worry, I'll make sure you get reassigned and get a really big raise. But I need you to do one last thing for me. Book a flight to Ireland. Make it for Sunday, if you can. I have to go out and visit my parents tomorrow."

"You're going back to Ireland so soon? Is everything all right? Did something happen with the job over there?"

"Something did happen." Jordan smiled. "I met this incredible Irishman named Danny Quinn. And I'm madly in love with him."

JORDAN GROANED SOFTLY, then sat up and turned on the bedside lamp. She picked up her pillow and punched it, then finally tossed it on the floor. She'd been trying to go to sleep for the past hour, desperate to at least get some rest before she had to face her mother in the morning.

She wanted to look fresh and beautiful and unimaginably happy when she saw her parents. Not tired and haggard and grumpy. Quitting her job had really been the easy part. Explaining to her mother why she couldn't marry one of the suitable bachelors available on the east coast would be the difficult part.

She'd tried calling Danny three times, but his voice mail had picked up each time. She'd started to worry that he'd changed his mind about her, that leaving had been a critical mistake. Jordan had even thought about calling the pub, for they'd know where he was. But in the end, she'd decided to give it another day and try him in the morning.

She imagined her homecoming in Ballykirk. She'd surprise him at the smithy. He'd be all hot and dirty and she'd throw herself into his arms and admit that she'd fallen in love with him and would never leave him again. And then they'd kiss and their life together would begin.

Occasionally, she'd think about a more gloomy scenario, still nagged by tiny slivers of doubt. She'd return, knock on his cottage door and find some gorgeous, half-naked woman in his bed.

Saying "I love you" was going to be a risk, but Jordan had decided that it was well worth it. After all, she'd taken the biggest risk of all—quitting her job and uprooting her entire life. How much scarier could things get?

She reached over and turned off the lamp and closed

her eyes. But the buzzer at her door brought her upright. She scrambled out of bed and hurried to the front door of her apartment to answer the doorman's summons.

"Yes?"

"Miss Kennally, it's Arnie. I have a man down here who insists on seeing you. I told him that you were probably sleeping, but he wouldn't take no for an answer."

Her father. He'd obviously broken the news to her mother and now had come to try to convince her to stay. She'd half expected her mother to call her by now. Jordan considered refusing him entrance, but maybe it was better to talk to him. In truth, she was starting to feel a bit guilty. "I'll be right down," Jordan said.

She hurried back to the bedroom and grabbed her robe, then walked to the elevator. As she descended, she smiled to herself. For the first time in her life, she felt like a grown-up. She'd made a decision for herself and she was happy about it. Sure, she'd miss her work, but she was setting out on a whole new chapter in life.

The elevator doors opened in front of her and her breath caught in her throat. A disheveled Danny Quinn waited for her. A gasp slipped from her lips and she rubbed her eyes. This couldn't be right. What was he doing here?

"Hi," he said, shifting back and forth on his feet.

Jordan stepped out and looked around the empty lobby. Arnie sat at his desk, watching her surreptitiously. "What are you doing here?"

"I just have to say something and then I'll go if you want. I'm not sure that I really made things clear before you left."

"You flew all the way here to say something to me?"

"Yes. I didn't really get a chance to say it the right way. And then when I realized that, I followed you to the airport, but you had already boarded your plane and they wouldn't let me get on and talk to you. So I bought a ticket, but then our plane had to stop in Iceland because of mechanical problems. And when I got here, I realized that I didn't have your address, so it took me a while to track that down, but—"

"You're here," Jordan murmured, with a smile.

"When you left, everything was happening so fast and I know we didn't get the chance to really say all the things we wanted to. I was trying to act like it was no big deal. And then, after you left, I thought, what if she doesn't come back."

"I have a ticket for Sunday, Danny. I tried to call you and let you know. I'm all packed."

"Really?" he asked, a smile breaking across his face.

"Really," she said.

He reached out and smoothed his hand along her arm. "Does this mean I get to touch you anytime I want, and I can kiss you and lie next to you and wake up with you in my arms every day?"

"Definitely," Jordan said. "I've been trying to sleep and I can't because you're not there." She paused. "I've missed you so much."

"And what about your job and your family? Won't you miss all that?"

"Of course I will. But it won't matter. I think I was throwing myself into work because I didn't have anything better to do with my time. But now, all I want to do is spend my days and nights loving you."

"You want to live in Ireland?"

She nodded.

He yanked her into his arms and kissed her deeply, his hands furrowing through her hair as he molded her mouth to his. And as Jordan lost herself in the wave of sensation that washed over her body, she realized that she couldn't live without him. His strength…his affection…his smile…

When Danny drew back, he glanced over her shoulder. "Can we maybe find someplace more private to talk? This really isn't the kind of thing that should happen in the lobby."

Jordan grabbed his hand and pulled him to the elevator. They stepped inside and she pushed the button for her floor. As soon as the door closed, Danny turned around and faced her, his gaze searching her face.

"I have something for you. But maybe I shouldn't do it here."

"What? You brought me a present?"

"I don't know if you'll want it. You might not even like it." He reached into his pocket and pulled out a ring, a beautiful antique ring with a small ruby set in a Victorian filigree.

"It was my great-grandmother's," he said. "My mum gave it to me when I told her that I was coming to see you." He drew a deep breath. "I promise that I will do everything in my power to make our lives together perfect."

The elevator door opened and Danny winced. "I should have waited. This isn't romantic."

Jordan laughed. "Oh, yes, it is." She took his hand and drew him out of the elevator. "Keep going. I'm listening."

"In the hallway?"

"All right." She ran ahead to her apartment door and by the time she got it unlocked he was behind her, his hands wrapped around her waist.

"Here?" she asked.

"No," he said, glancing around her apartment. He pointed to the sofa in the living room. "There."

When she was finally seated, Danny knelt in front of her. "All right. Here it is. Jordan, I love you. I think I fell in love with you the moment I first saw you. I know I fell in love with you the moment I kissed you."

She stared at him, wide-eyed, her hands clutched in her lap. Jordan tried to maintain a calm facade, but her heart was beating so hard it felt as though it might burst out of her chest.

"I'm willing to work hard. I'll do whatever it takes. I'm not sure I can give you what you have here, but I will make you happy. I can move to New York if that's what you want. You'll never have a day of regret, I promise."

"I know," she said. "And what about the ring?"

"Shite, the ring," he muttered, patting his pockets. "The ring. It's not something fancy, but it's a promise."

"A promise is good. And I don't need anything fancy."

He pulled the ring out of his pocket and slipped it on her finger, then pressed his lips to the back of her hand. "I want you in my life, Jordan. Forever."

"You have me," she murmured, running her fingers through his hair. "For as long as you want me." Jordan stood up in front of him and untied the belt of her robe. She shrugged out of it, letting it drop to the floor at her feet. Then she reached for the bottom of her nightgown. Grabbing the hem, she pulled it over her head and tossed it aside.

Danny reached out and splayed his hand across her stomach. "Are you trying to seduce me?" he asked.

Jordan smoothed her hand over his cheek. "Yes, I am."

"Don't you think we should talk about this a little more?"

She slowly shook her head. "We can talk later. I want to make love to the man I love."

He pulled her close and pressed his face into her stomach. "Promise me something, Jordan."

Furrowing her fingers through his hair, she tipped his gaze up to meet hers. "Anything."

"Promise we'll be together forever."

"I promise," she said, pulling him to his feet.

Danny stood to remove his clothes. When he was naked, he grabbed her waist and they tumbled onto the sofa in a tangle of limbs. When his mouth found hers, Jordan knew this was the only thing she needed in life. Danny Quinn—his heart, his soul, his body, his love.

Maybe there *had* been fairies at work in Ireland, she mused. After all, they'd found her the man of her dreams.

* * * * *

PASSION

For a spicier, decidedly hotter read—
these are your destination for romances!

COMING NEXT MONTH
AVAILABLE NOVEMBER 22, 2011

#651 MERRY CHRISTMAS, BABY
Vicki Lewis Thompson,
Jennifer LaBrecque,
Rhonda Nelson

#652 RED-HOT SANTA
Uniformly Hot!
Tori Carrington

#653 THE MIGHTY QUINNS: KELLAN
The Mighty Quinns
Kate Hoffmann

#654 IT HAPPENED ONE CHRISTMAS
The Wrong Bed
Leslie Kelly

#655 SEXY SILENT NIGHTS
Forbidden Fantasies
Cara Summers

#656 SEX, LIES, AND MISTLETOE
Undercover Operatives
Tawny Weber

You can find more information on upcoming Harlequin® titles,
free excerpts and more at www.HarlequinInsideRomance.com.

HBCNM1111

REQUEST YOUR FREE BOOKS!
2 FREE NOVELS PLUS 2 FREE GIFTS!

Harlequin *Blaze*™

red-hot reads!

Lucy Flemming and Ross Mitchell shared a magical,
sexy Christmas weekend together six years ago.
This Christmas, history may repeat itself when they find
themselves stranded in a major snowstorm...
and alone at last.

Read on for a sneak peek from
IT HAPPENED ONE CHRISTMAS
by Leslie Kelly.

Available December 2011, only from Harlequin® Blaze™.

EYEING THE GRAY, THICK SKY through the expansive wall of windows, Lucy began to pack up her photography gear. The Christmas party was winding down, only a dozen or so people remaining on this floor, which had been transformed from cubicles and meeting rooms to a holiday funland. She smiled at those nearest to her, then, seeing the glances at her silly elf hat, she reached up to tug it off her head.

Before she could do it, however, she heard a voice. A deep, male voice—smooth and sexy, and so not Santa's.

"I appreciate you filling in on such short notice. I've heard you do a terrific job."

Lucy didn't turn around, letting her brain process what she was hearing. Her whole body had stiffened, the hairs on the back of her neck standing up, her skin tightening into tiny goose bumps. Because that voice sounded so familiar. *Impossibly* familiar.

It can't be.

"It sounds like the kids had a great time."

Unable to stop herself, Lucy began to turn around, wondering if her ears—and all her other senses—were deceiving her. After all, six years was a long time, the mind could play tricks. What were the odds that she'd bump into *him,* here? And today of all days. December 23.

Six years exactly. Was that really possible?

One look—and the accompanying frantic thudding of her heart—and she knew her ears and brain were working just fine. Because it was *him.*

"Oh, my God," he whispered, shocked, frozen, staring as thoroughly as she was. "Lucy?"

She nodded slowly, not taking her eyes off him, wondering why the years had made him even more attractive than ever. It didn't seem fair. Not when she'd spent the past six years thinking he must have started losing that thick, golden-brown hair, or added a spare tire to that trim, muscular form.

No.

The man was gorgeous. Truly, without-a-doubt, mouthwateringly handsome, every bit as hot as he'd been the first time she'd laid eyes on him. She'd been twenty-two, he one year older.

They'd shared an amazing holiday season.

And had never seen one another again.

Until now.

Find out what happens in
IT HAPPENED ONE CHRISTMAS
by Leslie Kelly.
Available December 2011, only from Harlequin® Blaze™

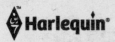
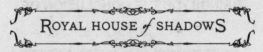